Darker Parker

Paperback edition published in 2021.

Author I.J Hidee

Edition and correction 2021 © I.J Hidee

The moral rights of the author have been asserted.

ISBN 9781085806367

Darker

Parker

☆ I.J Hidee ☆

For the lonely, the lost, the loved

Chapter 1: The Little Things

Christmas break started. Greg came over to fix the pipes. I thought it was so kind of him to help us get warm water running, but Parker simply rolled his eyes and said that Greg was afraid of getting fined. I bought Greg a small Christmas gift. It was a mug with his name printed on it. I gave it to Greg, and he seemed happy but apologized. I thought when someone received a gift; they said thank you. I forgave him.

Parker, Freddie, and Zev came over to my house. We were sitting in the living room, chatting and eating snacks. I was curled up beside Parker who shared a blanket with me. He held my hand, rubbing his thumb in circular motions over the back of my hand.

"Greg finally fixed the pipes," Zev laughed.

"Took him long enough," Parker grumbled.

"I like Greg," I said, and Parker sighed, resting his head on my small shoulder.

"This is why I worry about you," he murmured.

"What are you guys planning on doing for the holidays?" Zev asked. I felt Parker stiffen beside me, and he shifted his gaze. Freddie cleared his voice and broke the strange silence.

"I'm leaving the city to see my grandparents," Freddie said.

"I'm heading back to my hometown to see my parents," I answered.

"I'll probably spend Christmas with my old man," Parker shrugged.

"Are you guys free during the first week of vacation? Maybe we can do something together," Zev suggested. "My family is throwing a Christmas party on December 22nd. You can invite your parents if you want."

"On the 22nd? Christmas Eve is on the 23rd," Freddie said. Zev shrugged.

"We have this strange tradition of celebrating Christmas early."

Then he grinned.

"You can invite your mama," he said, and then shifted his gaze towards Parker. "And you can invite your daddio."

Parker and Freddie scowled.

"Are you trying to matchmake our parents?" Parker scowled.

"Well, they're both single, aren't they?" Zev chirped.

"That would mean I'd have to be Parker's stepbrother," Freddie said, shivering at the thought. "I'd rather die."

"Ditto."

"My ma' likes making new friends; it'd be nice if you could bring your mom. Are you guys coming on the 22nd?"

"If there's food, I'll be there," Parker said, and Zev grinned.

"Great! She loves it when I bring home good-looking guys," he chuckled. Zev knew how to make situations less awkward while still making them awkward. "Speaking of food, I'm getting hungry. How about we make dinner?"

Parker and Zev grabbed their coats and went to the groceries to buy some ingredients while Freddie and I went to the kitchen to peel potatoes.

"Freddie?" I said as I scrubbed the potato.

"Mhm?"

"Why was Parker upset when Zev asked us about the holidays?"

Freddie licked his lips, quiet for a moment.

"He used to spend winter break with his ex-boyfriend. You know, the one who passed away."

"Oh."

"He hasn't told you anything about him?"

I shook my head.

"I think he's still hurt," I murmured. "Parker is so nice to me. Whenever I have problems, he tries his best to be there for me. He buys me food and watches movies during my bad days, but he never tells me when he's not okay."

"Parker doesn't open up easily. He's scared of getting attached because he doesn't want to get hurt. You'll have to be a little patient, but you two have all the time in the world. I've seen the way Parker is around you, and even if you think you aren't doing anything, you're doing more than anyone else ever has. He's happy. *You* make him happy."

I made Parker happy. Freddie's words made me smile.

"How is it going with you and your boyfriend?" I asked. Freddie didn't talk much about him anymore, and we still hadn't met him. The three of us thought they had broken up until Freddie mentioned going on a date with him a few days ago.

"We got into another fight," he admitted. I frowned.

"A big one?"

"No, not really." He sounded unsure. "He was upset about something, but I'm sure it'll blow over."
"If you need someone to talk to, I'm here. I'm not a great talker, but I'm a good listener."

Freddie's brown eyes turned towards me, and he smiled. He smiled, but he looked sad.

"Thank you, Conan."

A little later, we heard the front door open, and Parker and Zev joined us. Zev took out the vegetable and meat from the grocery bag while Parker came over to help us peel the potatoes.

"Parker, you're supposed to peel the skin, not the entire potato," Freddie said, frowning at the chunks of potato in the sink.

"You're the one with the peeler. It's hard to peel with a knife," Parker growled.

"Conan doesn't seem to have a problem," Freddie smirked.

Parker splashed water at Freddie's face. He yelped and Parker snickered evilly. Freddie threw his half-peeled potato at Parker. I frowned and ran after the potato rolling across the kitchen floor. When I stood up, Parker and Freddie were wrestling and bickering. Freddie's neck was locked under Parker's armpit. They were such good friends.

Parker was laughing until he noticed something on Freddie's arm. He pulled up Freddie's sleeve, and our eyes widened at the purple bruises on his pale skin.

"Where'd you get these?" he asked firmly.

Freddie pushed him away, quickly pulling his sleeves down.

"I fell down the stairs."

Parker blinked.

"Are you dumb or are you dumb?"

"It was dark, and I wasn't paying attention to the steps. I'll ask Greg to fix the elevator," Freddie grumbled, looking away to focus on peeling the potatoes, but the back of his neck and ears burned bright red.

Parker didn't seem convinced, but before he could start interrogating Freddie, Zev turned on some music. He began humming along to the rhythm, swaying his hips side-to-side as he cut the vegetables. He picked up a metal spoon and sang. It wasn't just a gentle hum; he sang as if he was on stage. Freddie stared at him blankly, Parker cringed with a scowl, and I smiled. And that's how it all began. Zev passed the metal spoon to Freddie, who shook his head.

"Oh, come on, sing with me," Zev insisted. Freddie hesitated at first but took the metal spoon and mumbled the lyrics. Zev then passed the spoon to Parker who rolled his eyes.

"This is so stupid," he muttered under his breath, but to our surprise, he took the spoon and sang. What shocked us even more was that he knew the lyrics by heart. Parker's nice, deep voice matched the melody, and he sang so well.

Zev then passed me the spoon. I knew some of the words, not all of them, but enough to sing some parts. My singing voice wasn't as nice as Parker's, but my friends didn't seem to care. They were too busy dancing.

Zev played against his imaginary guitar, while Freddie started doing a funny little dance, while Parker pretended to play the drums. Everything was so silly, so absurd, and that was what made everything so fun.

Zev then collapsed on his knees, pulling his imaginary guitar to his chest and doing a solo. He scrunched his face, strumming his imaginary pick against the imaginary strings, playing with all his heart and might. Parker, Freddie, and I cheered his name and clapped like fanboys at their favorite rock' n' roll concert.

And the night continued like that, singing, laughing, giggling. We were four college students, silly, young, naive; throwing potatoes and splashing water, arguing and laughing, eating and drinking, playing and singing. We were happy. It was a simple but perfect night.

Chapter 2: A Merry Christmas

It was Christmas Eve. Well, it was Christmas Eve for Zev's family. December 22nd arrived, and Parker, Freddie, and I were getting ready to go to Zev's house. Parker's dad and Freddie's mom were also going and said they'd meet us there.

We had a dress code: wear anything red, white, or green, and Zev said we'd get bonus candy if we wore something sparkly. After changing, I went upstairs to join Parker and Freddie. Parker was wearing all black, but he wore a bracelet with green beads, so I guess that counted. Freddie was dressed in a bright red sweater.

"Guess what?" I said excitedly. "Greg said he fixed the elevator for us."

Parker raised his brows. "That old fucker?"

"Language," Freddie snapped.

"Sure, sure," Parker sighed, lazily waving his hand at him. He pressed the elevator button and our eyes widened in surprise when a neon orange number appeared on the panel with the arrow sign pointing up.

"It's actually working," Parker said, astonished.

"It's a Christmas miracle," Freddie gasped.

We stood there, shocked when we heard a 'DING.' The metal doors slid open.

"Someone pinch me," Freddie uttered. The three of us stepped in, and I pressed the first floor. The metal doors closed and the elevator began going down. But then it ground to a stop. Parker pressed the buttons on the panel, but the elevator wouldn't respond. And then the dim light above us flickered off, and we were left in the dark.

"I knew it was too good to be true," we heard Parker grumble. He turned on his phone's flashlight.

"Dandelion, hold this for me," Parker said, handing me his phone. I took it and Parker slid the tip of fingers into the small gap between the metal doors. He let out a grunt when he forced them open, but there was a concrete wall in front of us. We were stuck between two floors.

"This is what he calls fixed?" Parker groaned in despair. "I'm going to kill him."

"I'll try calling him," Freddie said, dialing a number into his phone. It began ringing, and then someone picked up. "Hey, Gre-"

"Hello! This is Greg Pinochet's number, landlord of the 2B building in the Big City. Unfortunately, I am currently unavailable at the moment, but I promise to get back to you A.S.A.P! If it's an urgent matter, please leave me a message after the beep."

BEEEEEP.

Parker snatched the phone out of Freddie's hand.

"You better get your ass over here A.S.A.P before I break your damn kneecaps, ya old man," he snapped. He angrily hung up, shoving the phone against Freddie's chest who staggered back from the impact. We waited thirty minutes for Greg to call us back, but it seemed like he wasn't going to call us A.S.A.P.

"We're going to be late for the party," Freddie frowned.

"Maybe we can get out through the emergency escape," I suggested, pointing at the ceiling.

"Okay, I'll help you two up," Parker said. "Who wants to go first?"

Freddie volunteered. Parker crouched down and Freddie climbed onto his shoulders. It reminded me of the last time we pulled a stunt like this when Parker dangled Freddie off the roof of a building to get his shoe. I realized I had made so many nice memories with my friends.

"Can you reach the top?" Parker asked.

"Yup," Freddie said, pulling the metal door open. He grabbed the ledge and pulled himself up. Freddie used his upper strength to wiggle up the small door, kicking Parker in the face by accident.

"You're up next, Conan," he said, swatting Freddie's foot away. He crouched down and I climbed onto his shoulders. He held my hands when he stood up. His warmth seeped into my skin, and I felt a little less afraid.

"You okay?" Parker asked, looking up at me with worried eyes.

"Yes," I said. And I was.

Freddie's head appeared from the hole above.

"Come on, Conan, I'll help you up," he grinned. I held onto the ledge but didn't have the upper strength to pull myself up, so Parker pushed me up while Freddie pulled me out. When I climbed onto the elevator, it was Parker's turn. Parker leaped and caught the ledge of the open ceiling, swiftly pulling himself up with a grunt.

We climbed up the rusty, metal ladder that led to the roof. A gentle gust of wind greeted us when Freddie's pushed open the door. We climbed out on the snowy roof, our eyes widening at the view below. I ran up to the ledge with an excited smile.

Our apartment wasn't tall enough to see the entire city, but we still had a nice view of the city lights. The Big City was covered in a blanket of snow, decorated with bright lights that ornamented the streets.

"Who knew the crappy building had such a nice view?" Parker snorted, standing beside me.

"Hey, how about I take a picture of you two?" Freddie suggested. He already had his phone out. "Come on Parker, smile a bit!"

"I am," he snapped. I looked up at him and laughed, holding his hand and giving him a small squeeze.

"Thank you for everything," I whispered to him. Parker's eyes widened, and he turned his head away. He was blushing.

"Alright ya love birds. One, two, three, say, Freddie!"

"Freddieeee!" I cheered, and he snapped the picture. We took more pictures before heading downstairs. As we left the building, I ran up to Parker and Freddie and hugged them both. I didn't feel nauseous or sick.

"What's all this about?" Freddie chuckled.

"I just felt like it," I beamed. I'd like to hug them more often.

We arrived at Zev's house an hour late. When we told him what happened, he burst into laughter, laughing so hard he almost fell to the floor.

"That Greg guy really is something," he chuckled. "I can't believe you guys climbed up the emergency ladder."

"Don't make our guests stand at the door. Let them in," Zev's mother said. It struck me how young she looked, and when I told her she was beautiful, she laughed and told me to come over whenever I wanted. I also thanked her for giving birth to Zev.

"Conan being Conan," my friends sighed with a smile.

Zev's dad, uncle, aunts, and cousins were already sitting at the dinner table. I recognized Dr. Anderson who was sitting beside a lady wearing a formal suit. She had the same red hair as Freddie. She must be his mom.

We introduced ourselves and apologized for being late before sitting with them for dinner. We closed our eyes and said our prayers. Zev said his family was very religious, which worried Freddie at first, but Zev promised that they held no prejudice against the queer community.

Dinner was so much fun and full of life. The living room was filled with a hubbub of chatter and laughter. Zev's parents had fun passing around Zev's baby pictures and even let us keep some of them. After dessert, we decided to play some music. We sang, danced, and drank. Freddie was talking with Dr. Anderson and his mom about political issues until Zev grabbed his hand and pulled him onto his feet.

"Come on, Fred, dance with me!" Zev beamed, and for some reason, Freddie looked flustered. But he didn't turn down the offer, and they both hopped around and tried to follow the beat of the music but were too drunk to make coherent movements.

We then gave each other presents. I bought Zev's mother some caramel scented candles, I gave Freddie a book and Zev candy from all over the world. I bought Parker a scarf so he wouldn't get cold during the winter. When we finished exchanging presents and singing Christmas carols, we sat around the fireplace, drinking hot chocolate and roasting marshmallow. It was as if we were one big happy family. No matter what we looked like, where we were from, who we were, it felt like home.

"Why didn't you invite your boyfriend?" Zev asked, resting his head on Freddie's lap.

"He said he was busy."

"Are you two still fighting?"

"No."

Freddie was a terrible liar. Zev didn't seem happy, but he didn't ask further questions.

"I'm glad he didn't come. You deserve better," Zev whispered. Freddie smiled sadly, and the flames reflected red against his freckled face, but I was certain he was blushing.

"Uncle Conan?" Asked one of Zev's cousins "Could you get us some more marshmallows?"

"Yes, of course. Where are they?"

"In the lower cupboard in the kitchen," she beamed. I stood up and walked down the corridor, but someone grabbed my arm and pulled me aside. I staggered sideways, my eyes widening when Parker pushed me against the wall. He leaned forward for a kiss, but I stopped him.

"Parker," I frowned. "We can't do this here."

Parker sighed, and I could tell that he was slightly drunk. He pressed his forehead against my shoulder, tilting his head sideways to look at me. His dark hair fell over his beautiful forehead. Despite knowing him for months, it felt like I was seeing him for the first time. His breath was warm against my neck, and it sent tickles down my spine.

"Hey, Dandelion," he whispered. "Are you scared of me?"

The question surprised me.

"No, of course not," I murmured gently. He nodded with a small smile.

"Good."

He pulled away and ran his hand through my hair, tilting my head back. His lips were so close to mine.

"Can I kiss you?" He asked. I nodded, and I felt his lips immediately press against mine.

The kiss wasn't sweet or soft like the ones he's engaged in before. It was hard and claiming, and when his tongue touched mine, I could see the hunger in his eyes. And for some strange reason, if there even was some form of rationality left in my fuzzy mind, I wanted Parker to push further. I wanted him to be rougher. I wanted to experience the things he enjoyed and wanted to be part of a life I shied away from. Parker deepened the kiss, and I could taste champagne lingering on his tongue. He pressed against me and I felt a throbbing pulse between my legs. Embarrassed, I tried to hide my lower member.

"Parker," I whispered, but he removed my hands and let his hand wander up my inner thigh. My knees buckled and I clasped my hand over my mouth to stop a whimper from escaping.

"I'm sorry," I apologized. Parker took my hand and my eyes widened when he pressed my palm against his bulge. His pants tightened around his crotch, and he squeezed my hand around him. He felt big.

"Uncle Conan?" Called a voice. Parker quickly pulled away from me before Diana saw us. She blinked curiously.

"Uncle Conan, what are you doing?" she asked.

"Finding the marshmallows," I stammered.

"With uncle Parker?" She frowned.

"Ah yes, the marshmallows! Come on, Conan, let's go find them."

Parker quickly grabbed my hand and pulled me towards the kitchen. He let out a small sigh of relief when we were out of sight.

"That was a close one," he grumbled. We looked at each other, paused, then giggled ourselves silly. Parker held my hand and gave me a gentle squeeze, and the small gesture meant the world to me.

Chapter 3: The Butterfly Effect

The Christmas party ended. We were all too drunk to drive home. The parents put their kids to bed and took out some old mattresses and extra blankets and slept on the floor.

"Conan, you can sleep in the guest room," Zev whispered, cradling his cousin who slept in his arms. "I know you aren't comfortable when there are too many people."

I frowned, feeling bad. Everyone else was sleeping on the floor, even Dr. Anderson.

"Go on, have a good night's sleep," Zev said, giving me a gentle push with his hips.

"But-"

"G'night, Conan, and Merry Christmas," he said, tousling my hair before heading to the living room to tuck in his cousin. I hesitated at first but headed upstairs to the guest's room. When I opened the door, my eyes widened.

Parker was standing beside the bed, shirtless. His hair was still slightly wet from his shower. Beads of water ran down his abs, tracing down the curves of every muscle. His shoulder blades flexed when he picked up his sweater and my breath caught in my throat.

"Good evening, Parker," I murmured, staring at the wall. He laughed, and when I turned towards him again, he had already put his sweater on. I felt strangely disappointed.

"A good evening indeed," he said. "I'm exhausted."

I climbed onto the bed. It felt strange sleeping on someone else's bed, but I was glad Parker was beside me. He turned off the lights and lied down beside me, putting an arm around my waist and gently pulling me against his chest. His strength was staggering, and I could feel the muscles in his forearms flex when he pulled me closer, but he was careful with me. He felt warm and smelled nice. His lips were close to the nape of my neck and his warm breath sent tingles down my spine. A strange curling sensation hit my lower stomach. It wasn't unpleasant. Not at all. It was warm and tingling, reminding me of my first sip of bubbly champagne.

"Today was fun." I could hear the smile in his voice and relaxed a little.

"It was."

"I've never had a Christmas party like this," he chuckled.

"What were your Christmas parties like before?" I asked quietly. Parker was silent for a moment, and I wondered if my question was too personal.

"It was just me and my ex. Sometimes Dad was there, sometimes he wasn't," Parker replied. He was quiet for a second, perhaps for a handful of minutes, but I lost my sense of time whenever I was with Parker, especially when he held me like this.

"I didn't really care about winter break. It was simply a time when I could relax and stay home without having to worry about class or bio-chem, but Eden was different. Every year he'd insist on buying a tree and expensive decorations. He loved going out to eat on Christmas Eve and made me stay up with him until midnight so he could put up the star on the tip of our tree. He loved the holidays. Eden was so full of life and joy. It sometimes frustrated me how optimistic he was, and I'd sometimes wonder how someone so happy could exist. Yet, he was here. He existed. He lived."

Parker never spoke about his ex-boyfriend and hearing him talk about him now made me understand why. Parker suffered on his own and no matter how badly I wanted to make him feel better, some wounds couldn't be healed.

"Do you miss him?"

"Every day."

I wondered if I should feel jealous, but I didn't.

"Sorry, I'm kind of ruining the mood, aren't I?" he said. I shook my head.

"Why do you study bio-chem?" I asked. Another pause, another hesitation.

"For my dad," he replied.
"Because you want to make him proud?"

"Because I feel guilty. It's my fault Mom died. The least I can do is become someone she would have been proud of."

I turned to face him.

"I think you should be happy, Parker. Your parents want you to be happy. Eden would have wanted you to be happy. I want you to be happy."
"I can't be happy if you leave."

My chest tightened.

"You won't go, right? You'll stay by my side and love me the way you do right now. Tell me you will."

My heart ached. It ached for him. It ached for me. And then I remembered an excerpt from *The Iliad* that I once told him when he was on the bathroom floor in his apartment.

Everything is more beautiful because we are doomed. You will never be lovelier than you are now. We will never be here again.

Parked pulled me closer when I didn't reply, holding me desperately. There was no anger in his eyes, but pain and sorrow and an emotion so raw I couldn't quite name.

"Conan, I love you," he said, and the conviction and desperate plea in his voice made it impossible for me to doubt him. "Why won't you stay?"

"Have you ever heard of the butterfly effect?" I asked.
Parker furrowed his brows. "I have, but I don't know much about it."

"It's a theory in which people believe that the tiniest actions will influence the course of their entire life. Many factors play a part in us being here. Sometimes the factors are large: fear, death, life. Sometimes the factors are small, like a broken elevator, a sip of alcohol, or crossing the road. We are who we are because every moment of our life has brought us here. While we exist, every second matters," I murmured, looking into his deep dark eyes. "I was only twelve when it happened."

"When what happened?"

"When my uncle first touched me," I said. Parker's eyes widened. "It wasn't anything serious at first. He'd put his hand on my leg under the dinner table while he talked with my parents. No one knew but us. I didn't think much of it, but his hand would wander to places that made me uncomfortable. One time, I went to the bathroom to cry, and he followed me and told me he loved me but that I couldn't tell anyone."

My eyes fell to Parker's chest.

"I feel like I've become something broken, someone sick, a human who can't function properly but who still exists because that's what people do. They live. They don't like it, but they still live. It's a strange feeling," I murmured.

I smiled, and I realized why people smiled when they were sad. It was an external face, a defense mechanism, it was another lie to protect us from what weighed on our hearts and mind.

"That's why I came to the Big City. I wanted to live the life I would have lived if I were normal. I wanted to be happy, even if it were for just a day, I didn't want to be Conan the Victim anymore. I didn't want to depend on the doctors or the pills, and I didn't want the Dark Thoughts to control me. I'm so grateful that I met you, Parker. You, Freddie, Zev, Greg, Dr. Anderson, everyone. You're all so kind to me, and even though I feel broken, you've accepted me for who I am, and I don't think I could have asked for a greater gift."

I looked at Parker. The world had been such a scary place before I met him, but now I understood why life was beautiful. Life was painful, it caused suffering; it was terrible, but in life, I saw more than misery. In life, I saw Parker, and in Parker, I saw happiness.

"You deserve to be happy," I told him. "And I hope with all my heart that there is someone in this world who can exist with you."

"Why can't that someone be you?" he pressed. "You want me to be happy, but you know what? *You* make me happy. I'm going to keep loving you. I'm going to make sure you stay by my side, that you eat your food, that you go to class, that you see your friends because yes, Conan, you have friends who love you so much. You're going to meet new people, visit new places, see the world. You're going to live and you're going to be happy."

I opened my mouth to say something, but he spoke first.
"I'm going to be selfish with you. I'm going to be so selfish that I'm going to make you happy. I'll make you want to stay. I'll make you regret even thinking about leaving. You're going to take lots of pictures," he said, and as he did, tears spilled down his face. "You're going to read lots of books, you're going to tell me the different theories you've come up with, you're going to take warm showers in our crappy apartment building, and you're going to make us our favorite turkey sandwich every week. You're going to celebrate Christmas next year and the one after. You're going to have a wonderful life, Conan."

I looked at him with a frown. And as if he was afraid to hear my answer, he kissed me. He kissed me as if he couldn't have done anything else. The second our lips touched; I couldn't help but relive every moment we've spent together. I was torn between wanting him and saving him, but love was paradoxical in that way. You loved so much it hurt.

Parker's hands moved up my waist, then my shoulders, then up to my neck and around my jaw. He kissed me, so desperately, so intensely. He kissed me as if it were our last.

Parker then pulled away, breathing hard. I realized that my arms were wrapped around his neck and that my body had unconsciously gravitated towards him. His thumbs brushed over my inner thighs and I felt an electric shock jolt through me. Parker rested his hands on my hips, his lips on my collarbone, my neck, then he kissed my ear. His breath felt hot against my skin, and I could feel my pulse pounding and my heart crashing under his touch.

For a second, I thought he'd go further, and I was surprised to find myself disappointed when he didn't. Instead, we looked at each other, breathing hard with clashing emotions lodged in our hearts. He kissed my cheek and rested his forehead against my thin shoulder like a defeated soldier.

"Don't forget me," he whispered.

Afterward, I would replay that moment and cry. My biggest regret in life was never asking him to return the promise — to never forget.

Chapter 4: Spiraling Down

Classes started again in January. Blankets of snow rested upon the park benches and tree branches, and as the morning sun rose, the frost turned into sparkling crystals vibrant with natural glitter. I let out a long breath to watch the mist rise and vanish into the wintry air. I loved doing this since I was little; to watch something vanish before my eyes.

During the first weekend, Ryan and I finally met. He said his house was under renovation, so I invited him to my mine for rehearsal. When I opened the door, he stood at the entrance with a smile. His hair and shoulders were covered in snow.

"Don't laugh. I didn't think it'd snow so much," he sulked.

"Hello, Ryan. It's okay. Life is unpredictable."

I pressed on the tip of my toes to help remove the layer of white on his hair. He lowered his head so I could reach it easily, and he looked at me through his thick lashes. His blue eyes seemed brighter than before. His lips pressed into a smile when I patted away the snow on his head.

"It's nice to see you again," he murmured. I realized it had been almost a month since I hadn't seen him. "You look better."

I wondered what he meant by better. Perhaps it was a new trendy way of complimenting someone. I made a mental note to ask Freddie later.

"Merry Christmas and happy new year, even though I'm a little late," I said.

"Thanks, Conan. I hope this year everything you wanted will come true," he winked.

"I'll hang your coat in the living room so it can dry," I suggested. Ryan nodded and shrugged off his coat. When he placed it in my hands, I fell forward. It was so heavy. Or perhaps I was too weak. Perhaps I should eat more protein as Parker suggested. Zev knew how to cook the juiciest chicken breasts, perhaps I could ask him for his recipe. While I hung Ryan's coat, I thought of my friends and realized how lucky I was to have them.

"The elevator is broken," Ryan noted.

"Oh yes, Greg said he'd fix it ASAP." I paused. "Well, he fixed it last month, but it broke, and my friends and I had to climb up the emergency hatch. But I'm sure Greg will fix it again soon. Though, I don't think his notion of 'soon' is the same as ours. Do you think he perceives time through a different reality?"

Ryan's brow knitted.

"Um, I'm not too sure," he admitted.

After talking about our Christmas and what we had done during the holidays, we practiced our lines together. Ryan helped me with the intonations and pauses, teaching me how to convey emotions without sounding too choppy or dramatic. He also taught me how to work on my facial expressions, and I had so much fun. When he asked me to scowl, I imagined Parker's face. I was impressed by how knowledgeable Ryan was in acting and playwright, and when I complimented him, he blushed.

We took a break after two hours of practicing. I asked him if he'd like some coffee or tea, and he chose tea, so I went to boil some water.

"Would you like the Christmas cinnamon special?" I asked, setting several boxes in front of him. "I also have jasmine and mint tea."

"I'll try the Christmas special," he smiled, and I nodded. He pulled out a chair and sat down, his eyes studying my house.

"It's nice and cozy here," he murmured, but his eyes stopped on the pack of cigarettes on the counter. "I didn't know you smoked."

"Oh, I don't. It's Parker's," I told him, giving him the mug. "He always leaves his stuff here."

Ryan pursed his lips. "You two live together?"

"He lives upstairs. So does Freddie," I smiled. "Freddie is my best friend, and so is Zev."

As I made the tea, I could feel Ryan stare at me. Did I sound too arrogant? Perhaps he thought I was bragging… Maybe I should say something else. Parker was good at making conversations and changing topics. How did he do it so easily? Should I talk about a movie? A play? Maybe a book? While my mind digressed, Ryan spoke first.

"Are you close to Parker?"

I blinked at him. "Yes, he lives right above me. I think there's an eight-meter distance that separates his house from mine."

Ryan chuckled, shaking his head.

"No, I wasn't talking about the distance between your houses," he said, taking the mug and pressing his hands against it to warm his hands. Ryan smiled a strange sort of smile. He opened his mouth. Closed it. Pried it open again.

"You said you were homophobic, so correct me if I'm wrong, but are you dating Parker?" he asked, biting his lower lip. The question surprised me.

"Yes, I'm dating Parker," I said. Ryan's jaw tightened.

"Since when?" he asked, his voice suddenly bitter.

"Since December," I told him.

"You flirted with me while dating Parker?" Ryan asked with a twisted smirk. My eyes widened.

"I wasn't flirting," I frowned, confused by the accusation.

"You said I was handsome," he snapped. I felt myself shrink.

"Because it's true," I whispered, and Ryan looked like he wanted to hit me. He was handsome, it was factual information like any other. The sky was blue, the weather was cold, Ryan was handsome, they were simply facts.

"Are you okay?" I asked.

Ryan ran a hand through his hair, staring at the table before glaring at me.

"What do you see in him? He smokes and drinks and sleeps with anyone who'll spread their legs for him."

I flinched at his words, but he said nothing and waited for me to reply. I felt as if I was being scolded by Uncle Bo. Thinking of him made me squirm, and I suddenly didn't feel safe in my house. I wanted to go to Parker. He was only a few steps away. All I'd have to do was get up and walk up a flight of stairs and knock on his doors, and the world would be okay again. But I didn't. Because Ryan wasn't Uncle Bo and I promised myself to try and fight back the Dark Thoughts this year.

"Parker isn't like that," I murmured.

"I'm really disappointed," Ryan sighed. Although his appearance remained the same, something inside Ryann had shifted. His blue eyes were as cold as the first winter frost, and I felt my stomach twist into a knot.

"I'm sorry, I didn't mean to upset you," I frowned.

"I thought you were different, but you're just like the other fools in high school who worship people just for their looks. They could be an empty shell, but you'd still like them because they're hot. Isn't that right?"

Before I could reply, he cut me off.

"I mean, why else would you date Parker? All he sees in you is a small guy who'll be submissive for him in bed. Why can't you see that?"

Ryan's cruel words hurt. They hurt because I was reduced to sex. I was back to being a disposable body that existed only to please others. I was back to what Uncle Bo made me.

I tried to smile. "Parker is really kind and patient."

"Yeah, because he wants to sleep with you."

'*Conan, do you know what you are?*' a voice whispered.

I remembered being pressed against the wall. I remembered trying to grasp for something, but the wall was flat, and there was nothing to hold onto but air. I was too afraid to speak, too scared to move, and when Uncle Bo lowered his lips to my ear, I felt sick.

'You're a whore.'

I had never heard the word at that time. I was too young. But even though it was the first time, some part of me knew.

"We haven't slept together," I quickly said, in hopes to convince him that Parker wasn't the way he thought he was.

His brows shot up. "You haven't?"

"No," I murmured, squeezing my hands. Ryan bit his lip, running a hand through his hair.

"Let's get back to rehearsal."

I didn't want to rehearse anymore. I wanted him to leave, and I wanted to find Parker.

"Okay," I murmured. Ryan didn't touch the Christmas cinnamon tea and stood up. I followed him to the living room. Ryan flipped through the script.

"We'll practice act five, scene one."

My stomach curled.

"The kiss scene?" I squeaked. We had never practiced that scene before. I told Ryan I wasn't ready, and he said we could wait until later. Why did he change his mind? Was he punishing me?

"We have to practice for the play. We only have a month left before our real performance. Besides, I'm sure you've practiced enough kissing with Parker."

"I don't think I'm ready," I told him.

"Stop being selfish, Conan, you're going to ruin the play for everyone."

Everyone was working so hard to make the play a success. The decorations, the music, the mise-en-scène... Guilt clung to my shoulders.

"Okay," I said, squeezing my hands to reassure myself. "Okay, we'll do the scene. But can we stop at the kissing part? I have to ask Parker first."

"Sure, whatever," he said. I tried to focus on my lines, remembering the advice Ryan had given me.

This is just acting, Conan. Nothing bad will happen.

"Clark, if you love me, I'll be in your heart. If you hate me, I'll be in your mind. Love me or hate me, but don't push me away," Ryan said.

"Hate," I said. My voice cracked, and he narrowed his eyes, so I quickly cleared my voice.

You can do this, Conan. Focus.

"Hate," I repeated, feigning confidence. "Such a word does not exist when I look at you."

"Then prove it," he said, taking a step forward. I unconsciously stepped back, my back pressing against the wall behind me. Ryan reached out, his fingers curling around my jaw and raising my face. "Prove that you love me with a kiss."

Everything spun, and the air felt damp. Ryan's body pressed so close to mine I could feel his heat radiate against me. I didn't like it. Ryan's hand coiled around my waist like a snake, and his head moved closer towards mine. Before our lips could touch, I turned my face away, fighting back the urge to vomit.

"Ryan," I spoke frantically. "You said we wouldn't kiss. Can we stop? Parker-"

"Do you know how badly I want you?" Ryan whispered into my ear. Those weren't the lines in our script. I tried to squirm away, but he was too strong and wouldn't let me go. He tried to kiss me again, but I turned my face the other way, so he pulled down the collar of my shirt, exposing my neck and shoulder. My eyes shot wide open as he pressed his lips against my collarbone. A sharp pain shot through me when he bit into my flesh, sucking hard against my skin.

"Please, Ryan, stop," I begged him, trying to push him away, but he only tightened his grip, sinking his teeth into my skin until they sunk into my bones. One of his hands slipped up my shirt while the other groped my thigh, and I wanted to scream for help but when I opened my mouth, he clasped a hand over my lips.

"Don't fight it, Conan. If you stay still, it'll be over soon," he whispered. Or perhaps it was the Dark Thoughts speaking. I couldn't tell anymore.

My body went numb and my mind went blank. I couldn't remember what happened afterward, but when I regained consciousness, I was lying on the cold, hard floor. Ryan was gone and so was his coat. How much time had gone by since he left? My clothes were still on my body, which I suppose was a good sign, but they were wrinkled and undone. I wasn't sure whether Ryan had stopped halfway or if this was the clumsy result of him trying to dress me again.

I stared at the ceiling, feeling empty. Then my phone rang. I wasn't sure how I had found the strength or courage to answer it, but I did.

"Hey, Conan!" It was Freddie's cheerful, bright voice.

I tried to say something, but tears filled my eyes. A roar of emotions banged against my chest, and I wanted to hang up, but I knew if I did, I'd do something bad.

"Hello?" Freddie said.

I tried to sound normal, but I couldn't. I was shaking so badly; I could hardly keep the phone against my ear. I curled into a ball, hugging my knees against my chest for some reassurance.

"Freddie, I need help," I choked. I broke into sobs and wasn't sure if he could understand what I was saying.

"What's wrong, Conan? Where are you?" he asked frantically.

"Home. Can you come over, please?"

"Of course, I'll be down there in a sec."

"Don't tell Parker." I begged him. "Please, Freddie, please don't tell him."

"Stay put, I'm on my way," he said, and I could hear him running. I hung up and closed my eyes, pressing the phone against my chest.

Stay put, Conan. Stay put.

Chapter 5: Dear

Four days passed since the incident, but it felt like it was just yesterday. Freddie came over after I called him and found me shaking uncontrollably on the floor. He was about to call an ambulance, but I stopped him and made him promise not to. Freddie cried, begging me to let him call a doctor or the police, but I begged harder. From afar, I'm sure we looked silly: crying, shaking, arguing, then pleading. Freddie threatened to tell Parker, but I told him I'd never talk to him again if he did.

"Okay, fine," he answered angrily, wiping away his tears. "Have it your way. But Parker is going to find out sooner or later, and when he does, I won't be there to help you."

I knew that despite his cold words, he was wrong. Freddie would be there for me if Parker found out because that was the type of person he was. He was kind.

I asked if I could hold his hand, so he scolded me while holding my hand. To compensate for keeping that day a secret, Freddie made me tell him everything that happened, starting from why I used to feel sick whenever someone touched me. He stayed with me until I stopped shaking, which wasn't until late at night, but I was so thankful he was there. I didn't know what I would have done if he wasn't.

After that day, I lied to my friends and told them I needed to return to my hometown because of a family emergency. There was no emergency. But I didn't have the strength to get out of bed and socialize, or talk, or smile, or do any of the social activities humans did. Only Freddie knew the truth, but he promised not to tell.

On Monday, I wobbled to the bathroom, adjusting my clothes and straightening the wrinkles. I stiffened when I saw blood on my collarbone, and quickly turned on the sink to wash it off. Beneath the dried blood was a hickey and a bite mark that marred my skin in ugly colors.

My stomach curled and before I could stop myself, I vomited into the sink, expelling nothing. Saliva dripped from my lips, and I quickly washed my mouth. I pushed down the nausea and began scrubbing against the hickey as hard as I could, hoping it would go away. But it wouldn't go away, as if it were permanent, and scrubbing only irritated my skin even more. I gave up and went back to bed.

On Tuesday, I decided to take a bath, sitting in cold water, still scrubbing. It only made it worse. I caught a cold on Wednesday and couldn't find myself the strength or will to get out of bed. I lost all sense of place and time, and I stared at the ceiling, wondering how much longer this would go on. Not long, I hoped.

Parker and Zev had sent me messages and calls, but I turned off my phone and shut the world out, waiting for the week to end. I was waiting for the week to end me.
I placed my hand on my empty stomach, but I didn't feel hungry. On Thursday, I decided to write. I managed to find the strength to find a pen and my journal.

***

Dear,

By the time you read this, I will already be gone. But before I leave, I wanted to write you this letter. I'm not sure whether it is crueler to leave with or without a goodbye, but farewells have never been joyous to begin with. I don't know if you'll find this note, or if you'll read it, but I hope you do.

Firstly, I want you to know that no matter what happens; know that it isn't your fault. I've realized throughout my life that people blame themselves for things that aren't their fault. It's a strange mechanism us humans have, one that I'm familiar with. So if you read this, please know that you've done nothing wrong.

Secondly, I'd like to thank you. Before coming to the Big City, my life felt like a dark hole and a constant struggle. But after I met you, Freddie, Zev, and all the beautiful people of this world, I was able to experience true happiness. Words will never express how thankful I am to have met you. I will forever be grateful to the world for connecting our lives and intertwining our fates. I have many regrets, but you will never be one of them.

I don't know if I've mustered up the courage to tell you this — I hope I did — but know that I love you. They may be trivial words to you, perhaps they won't mean anything, but I have, and always will, love you.

Yours truly

Chapter 6: Live for Me

Then, on Friday, something happened. Someone knocked at the door, and my body stiffened when I heard Parker's frantic voice.

"Conan," he said, knocking harder. No, he was banging his fists against the door. "Conan open up. It's me, Parker."

What was he doing here?

"I know you're in there. Greg told me the water in your house has been running for the past few days, so don't act like you're dead."

He slammed his fists harder against the door.

"Conan, open the fucking door!"

I dragged my feet to the floor and stood up, feeling dizzy as soon as I did. I wobbled down the hallway, but my fingers stopped before they reached the doorknob. I heard him call my name, repeatedly, desperately, with only a thin wooden door separating us. I remained silent, and then the noise stopped. The knocking stopped and the world fell eerily quiet, and for a moment, I thought Parker had given up.

But Parker never gave up.

There was a soft thud that broke the silence as if he was pressing his forehead against the surface of the door.

"Please, Conan, open the door for me. It's me, Parker," he begged in a desperate plea. The tortured tone of his voice compelled me to do as he asked. I unlocked the door and pulled it open.

I didn't know what expression he had on his face because as soon as I opened the door, I stared at his chest. I knew it was Parker. He was wearing his favorite navy sweater which he let me borrow when I was cold, and I could easily recognize his firm and broad chest.

"Hello, Parker." My voice was stiff and mechanical like a pre-recorded CD. "How are you."

"Conan." his voice was no more than a whisper.

Parker walked past me and headed to the kitchen. I could hear him rummaging through my fridge. I stood at the entrance as he started making a sandwich. It was the fattest sandwich I had ever seen. I didn't think he was aware how many ingredients he was stuffing between the two loaves of bread. He was putting anything and everything he could find. Parker then pulled out a chair.

"Come here," he said, his voice strained. When I didn't move, his voice softened. "Will you please come here and sit?"

I knew something was wrong when Parker said please, but I nodded, too tired to argue. I sat down, and he set the plate in front of me.

"I know you're not hungry, but I made you a sandwich. Will you eat it for me?"

When I didn't answer, Parker ran his hands over his face, pacing back and forth, trying to calm himself. His fists were clenched so tightly, his knuckles were a ghostly pale shade. It looked like it hurt.

"Your phone was off," he said stiffly. He stood there, watching me. I felt so many things at once, that together, they combined to make nothing, a numbness, an absence of feeling caused by a surplus of feeling.

"Yes," was my sole answer.

"You said you were away. That you had a family emergency," he said, speaking as if someone was strangling him. I didn't answer.

"What's wrong, Conan? Did I do something wrong? Is there something that's bothering you? Tell me and I'll try to fix it. We'll find a way, Conan, I promise we will."

"I'm sorry."

"I'm not asking you to apologize," he said miserably. My silence shot down Parker's last ounce of patience.

"Conan, you have to fucking eat something!" he roared, pushing the plate towards me so violently, some of the ingredients plopped out. They didn't look like food, but substances that would make me even more miserable than I already was. Parker took in a tight breath.

"Do you want to eat something else? I can make you our favorite turkey sandwich. What about some warm soup? Zev taught me how to make porridge. It's not that hard, and it'll be easier to digest."

He tried to sound calm, but I knew he was reaching his limits. It was almost as if I wanted him to yell at me, to tell me how hopeless I was. I wanted him to hate me as much as I hated myself.

"I haven't eaten anything either. We can order food," his voice cracked, and when I looked up at him, I was shocked to see that he was crying. But Parker didn't seem to care. He was trying his best, he always was. Parker continued to try and fill the silence with empty words, desperate to get a response from me, "I can make something else for you, Conan, whatever you need. Just tell me and-"

"Parker," I answered, strangely calm.

Five days of absolute misery and all I needed was to see Parker. Being with Parker made me feel okay, but it didn't mean I was okay.

"Parker-"

Parker sank to his knees and held my hand in both of his. His face fell forward, and he looked like a miserable man praying in an empty church, holding my fingers between his palms so firmly, so desperately. He was shaking.

"Please, Conan, please," he begged. His request went further than the mere act of asking me to eat. He was begging for something that neither of us would name. And then he looked up, his dark midnight eyes unraveling endless sorrow.

"I'll stop drinking and smoking if you start eating," he whispered, and my eyes widened. What he meant was, '*I'll stop killing myself if you start living.*'

When I said nothing, he stood up, turning his face away so I couldn't see him.

"Porridge. I'll make you some porridge."

Parker went to the kitchen, and I could hear him turning on the stove and cutting vegetables. I decided to eat, and Parker watched me until the bowl of porridge was empty. He didn't ask me any more questions. He stayed the night but slept on the couch. When I woke up the next day, feeling less dizzy and drained, he had already prepared breakfast. Parker left me a note saying he had gone out to the pharmacy to get some medicine.

When he returned, I let him take my temperature. I had a fever, so he went out to buy more medicine. Parker then went to the living room to study. He brought his books and laptop to my house. I knew he didn't trust me on my own.

I wouldn't either. I pressed my lips together and decided to join him, sitting beside him on the couch.

"Parker?"

He didn't look up from his laptop.

"I'm sorry for being a handful," I murmured.

He was giving me the silent treatment.

"If you want to break up with me-"

Parker turned towards me, silencing me with a kiss. He pulled away, running his big hand through my hair and resting his forehead against mine.

"I love you, dandelion, but please shut up," was all he said.

"I love you too," I said. His eyes widened.

"What?"

"I love you, Parker." And I did. I loved him. No, 'love' wasn't enough to express what I felt for him. Parker was my neighbor, my best friend, my lover, and something much more than what words could define. I loved him more than I loved myself.

"And I'm sorry for being the way I am. I know you don't like it when I apologize, but I hope you can accept this apology. I'm sorry for hurting you so much," I said quietly. I knew that my misery also affected Parker. That was the ugly side of love. It was something beautifully tragic that linked two individuals to make one.

"I think you deserve someone better than me. You deserve someone more stable and less broken. So thank you for loving someone who isn't easy to love."

"You aren't easy to love, but you are worth every second of my life," he whispered, placing his hand on my cheek. His warmth spread and seeped into my skin, and I suddenly felt okay again. But when he leaned in to kiss me, he stopped.

"What's that on your neck?"

My eyes widened, but before I could stop him, he pulled down the collar of my shirt, revealing the bruised hickey near my thin collarbone. I quickly patched my hand over it, but Parker pulled my wrist away.

"What is that?" he asked, anger building in his eyes as he brushed his finger over the bruised area. I stiffened, quickly pulling away from him, and fell clumsily to the floor.

"It's just a rash," I lied feebly, adjusting my shirt.

"A rash with bite marks?"

"It's a bad rash," I mumbled.

"Then let me see your bad rash."

"I don't want to," I said, scrambling to my feet, but Parker stopped me.

"Conan," he said, his voice making me stiffen. "What happened to you?"

"Will you promise that you won't get mad?"

"I never get mad," he growled ironically.

"It was an accident."

"What are you talking about?"

"Ryan came over for rehearsal on Saturday and he wanted to do the kiss scene. And he..." I couldn't finish my sentence.

"Did you tell him you didn't want to do it?"

"I did, but he kissed my neck," I swallowed hard. "I'm sure he didn't know-"

"That fucking asshole!" he shouted. I blinked in surprise and when Parker was no longer standing in front of me, I panicked. He was already storming towards the door.

"Parker, where are you going?" I asked when he grabbed his coat.

"To kill him."

"Parker!" I shouted, running after him.

I tried to catch his arm, but he yanked away from me so abruptly, I almost lost my balance.

"Parker, stop!' I cried frantically, blocking the exit.

"No one touches you and gets away with it. Move," he ordered darkly.

"I'll talk to Ryan."

"You're not going anywhere near that piece of shit!" He bellowed.

Parker rarely swore when he was around me.

"I'm sure it was a misunderstanding," I tried to convince him. "Maybe I said something that gave him the wrong idea. It wasn't his fault."

"He almost fucking raped you, how is that not his fault?! And you know what's even worse? The fact that you're defending him. The fact that you think it's not his fault, but *yours*. You're blaming yourself for something that wasn't your fault, and it's driving me insane. Move aside so I can make sure Theatre Boy never lives another day standing on two feet," he said.

"Parker!" I cried, grabbing his arm. He pulled away and I lost my balance, crashing onto the floor and hurting my knees. But I grabbed his ankles and when he tried to walk forward, he tripped. I quickly held onto his legs like a koala and he tried to shake me off, but I clung to him.

I was glad the security cameras were broken and that Greg hadn't fixed them, because I'm sure we looked silly wrestling on the floor.

"Let go, Dandelion," he ordered.

"No!"

"Dandelion," he groaned, trying to peel me off his leg, but I climbed up his waist and wrapped my arms around his neck, pressing my face against the area between his neck and collarbone. I hugged him tightly.

"Don't go," I begged him.

The halls were silent. His back remained on the floor, but he gently wrapped his arms around me. His right hand pressed against the back of my head, gently touching my hair. I could feel his heart pounding against his chest.

"You're stronger than you look," he mumbled, but I knew it wasn't my physical strength that was holding him down.

"I want to kill him."

"But you won't."

Parker simply laughed. It was a sad, empty laughter.

"I'm going to call Freddie and Zev. They're worried about you," he said. He helped me up and told me to read a book while he made a few phone calls.

An hour later, Freddie and Zev came over. They didn't ask any questions, but I knew they knew.

"Hey, Conan, I brought you some candy," Zev grinned.

"Come on, Conan, let's watch a movie. I brought my DVDs," Freddie said, while Zev and Parker went to the living room to talk. They spoke so quietly, I didn't know what they were talking about, but it seemed serious because Zev wasn't smiling, and Zev always smiled. They returned but were now wearing their coats.

"Where are you guys going?" I asked nervously.

"We're going to get some fresh air," Parker said, but I didn't feel reassured. I looked towards Zev for an answer.

"We'll be back before you know it," he winked, tapping my nose.

"But-"

"Come on, let's watch Stuart Little," Freddie said, giving me a gentle tug. I caught him exchanging a glance with Parker and Zev, and could sense that the three of them were up to something. Reluctantly, I sat down beside Freddie on the couch.

"Where are they going?" I whispered. Freddie looked nervous for some reason, but he smiled and held my hand, giving me a gentle squeeze.

"Everything will be fine," he promised. I frowned. I craned my neck to see what Parker and Zev were doing, but they were gone.

Chapter 7: The New Romeo

As the movie was about to end, Freddie got a phone call. He left my side and went to the living room. I reached for the remote control and lowered the volume.

"Parker?" he answered. He stopped in his steps. "You what?!"

My brows knitted when Freddie tilted his head back with a groan.

"Yes, Conan is with me. Yes, he's fine. Yes, now will you stop worrying about him and start worrying about yourself? You said you'd control yourself!" Freddie snapped. "What about Zev?" There was a pause.

"Him too?!"

Freddie ran a frustrated hand through his ginger hair.

"No, *you* listen. If an officer asks you any questions, don't answer them. They can use whatever you say against you if they take this to court, and it'll be difficult for a lawyer to defend you. Wait until I arrive. We're on our way," he said, hanging up. He walked towards me with a heavy sigh.

"What happened?" I frowned.

"Parker and Zev are at the police station," he grumbled, and my eyes stretched wide open. "Come on, let's go."

I quickly grabbed my coat and scarf and followed him out the door. Freddie was busy making phone calls as we climbed down the stairs. We took his car and headed to the local police station.

"Are they okay?" I asked worriedly.

"I don't know. They're probably a little beaten up after fighting with Ryan," he grumbled. My chest tightened.

"But they should be fine," Freddie assured. "Unlike Ryan, they weren't sent to the hospital."

"Ryan's in the hospital?!" My kind imagined the worst-case scenario. "Is he dead?"

"Gosh, no!" Freddie said. "He's unconscious, that's all. Fortunately, a bystander called the police before those idiots could kill him."

He ran a frustrated hand through his hair.

"Imagine rotting in prison for someone so pathetic," he muttered angrily. I realized that Freddie wasn't worried about Ryan, but for Parker and Zev. Freddie clicked his tongue.

"Damn it, what the hell were they thinking?!"

I frowned and before I could say anything, Freddie cut me off.

"Conan don't blame yourself, *please.* No one is blaming you, so just don't," he said. "You can't spend your life apologizing for things that aren't your fault. If you want to help, then don't apologize to Parker when you see him. It'll drive him mad."

It's not my fault...

I nodded slowly.

"On the bright side, at least we don't have to make two trips to the police station. You can file a report against Ryan for sexual harassment."

My gaze fell to my lap, and Freddie frowned at my silence.

"You're going to file a report, right?" he inquired.

"I… I can't."

"Why not?"

"Please don't make me," I whispered. "It's already embarrassing enough."

"There's nothing to be embarrassing about," he murmured.

"Please, Freddie," I begged him quietly. "You won't make me tell them, right?"

Freddie pressed his lips together.

"If you don't testify yourself, then they won't even classify the case as an assault." Freddie paused. "I'm... I'm not going to force you, Conan. But..."

His voice drifted and I could see the sadness in his eyes.

But I'm disappointed in you, is what I expected him to say.

Freddie glanced at me, then sighed.

"I just wish the world was kinder to you," he murmured.

We arrived at the police station and my eyes widened when I saw Parker and Zev sitting in front of a desk with their hands cuffed in front of them. Parker's hair was a mess, and there was a cut on his lip. There was a scratch under his eye too. His knuckles were bruised and split open.

My eyes then shifted to Zev. His jaw was marred with a bruise, and his left eye was swollen, but he seemed to have fewer injuries than Parker. The policeman in front of them continued to interrogate them, but they took Freddie's advice and kept their lips sealed.

Freddie walked over towards them.

"Hi, hello," he quickly said. "Can I ask why these two are arrested?"

"They beat up an innocent bystander. They're here for questioning. Are you their father?"

Parker cackled.

"Does that redhead look like our father? I don't know if you've noticed, but my hair doesn't look like a tomato," Parker snorted. He jerked a thumb towards Zev. "And this guy is five shades darker than him."

At least Parker seemed the same despite his injuries.

"I thought I told you to call a close family member or companion," the officer deadpanned. Parker rolled his eyes.

"He *is* a close family member," he retorted. "And he also brought my companion."

Freddie and I blinked in surprise, but Parker remained nonchalant. The policeman sighed, rubbing his temples.

"I just want to know why you were beating up an innocent man."

"I don't think you have the right to qualify the beaten man as *innocent*," Freddie stated firmly. "How do you know he wasn't the one who caused the fight?"

"Which is why I'm questioning these two young men. I'd know what happened if they'd answer my questions," said the officer, looking irritated.

"They have the right to remain silent."

The officer laughed. "I am a man who represents the authority. I have the right to interrogate them."

"Then you should also know that they hold their Miranda rights. They'll see their lawyer before answering questions," Freddie said.

"You're telling me these kids have a lawyer?" he snorted.

"Mrs. Kelly," Freddie said curtly, handing him his mother's business card. Parker cocked a cut brow.

"You just wander around with that in your pockets?" He smirked. Freddie ignored him. His eyes remained on the police officer.

"Mrs. Kelly will be arriving in a few minutes."

So that's who he was on the phone with earlier?

Freddie's mom arrived ten minutes later. She was wearing a nicely tailored black and white suit. Her beautiful ginger hair flowed over her shoulders, and you could still see specks of her freckles despite the makeup. Freddie looked so much like her.

We were asked to wait outside the room while she and the officer discussed the situation. I glanced at Parker and Zev who avoided my gaze. Instead of scolding them or apologizing, I reached out and held their bruised hands, giving them a gentle squeeze.

"I'm glad you two are okay," was all I said.

"Zev!" Exclaimed a voice. We turned our heads and saw a beautiful girl with short, curly hair run towards us. She looked stunning, with bold, dark eyes and skin. She ran up to us and looked at Zev with worried eyes.

"Gosh, what happened to you?" She asked, putting her hand on her jaw.

"Hey, babe," Zev chuckled shyly. "I got into a small fight. But hey, what a great time and place to meet my friends."

Zev swiftly changed the subject, lowering the woman's hand from his face and intertwining his fingers around hers.

"Adah, meet Parker, Freddie, and Conan," he said, gesturing towards us. "Guys, meet my girlfriend, Adah."

I remembered Zev leaving to pick a call from his girlfriend the first time we met. She hadn't been able to come to the Christmas party because she was visiting her family in London. I didn't think the first time we'd meet would be at a police station.

"Hello!" I waved. "My name is Conan."

Adah had a beautiful smile, and two small dimples appeared in the center of her cheeks when she did.

"Hello, Conan," she said with a soothing British accent. "I've heard so much about you."

"Since when do you have a girlfriend?" Parker snorted.

"Since high school," Zev said.

"I'm really happy to meet you boys and I wish I could get to know you better, but can someone please explain to me why two of you are badly bruised?" Adah asked worriedly.

Zev quietly explained what happened, low enough for only us to hear. He didn't tell her everything that happened and said that Ryan had been bullying me and he and Parker went to teach him a lesson.

"I hope you kicked him hard in the shin," Adah said. "What idiot would pick on someone like Conan?"

We looked at her in surprise, but Zev smiled. It was a different smile. The way he looked at Adah was different too. I couldn't quite explain it, but you could tell he was very much in love with Adah.

"But was it really necessary to send him to a hospital?" She whispered.

"Absolutely," Parker snorted. "I regret nothing."

"He won't be walking anytime soon," Zev nodded.

"Then how is he going to play Romeo?" Adah asked. I looked at her, surprised, and she gave me a warm smile. "I told you, Zev loves talking about you three. He already bought us the tickets to your play."

Zev let out a nervous laugh.

"C'mon, babe, don't embarrass me in front of my friends," he mumbled. I've never seen him look so shy. He was normally the one making jokes and teasing others.

"They'll probably find a replacement," Freddie said.

"Wait, you mean Dandelion has to rehearse with another creep?" Parker growled.

"I was thinking of quitting," I admitted.

"But you put so much time and effort into memorizing your lines," Freddie frowned.

"I don't think I'm a very good Clark, and I don't know if I'm ready to rehearse with someone again. And there's a kiss scene…"

"I'll play Romeo."

We turned towards Parker in shock.

"Uh, since when were you into acting?" Freddie snorted.

"Since never. You think I want to prance around on stage wearing green leotards?"

"That's such a terrible stereotype," Freddie sighed.

"I like green," I smiled. "It reminds me of nature."

Adah laughed.

"I already love him," she said to Zev, which made me blush.

"You're really going to play Romeo?" Freddie asked. Parker turned towards me.

"If I play Romeo, will you play Clark?" He asked. I was much more comfortable around Parker, and I knew I'd be okay kissing him.

"But the play is in two weeks, and there are lots of lines to memorize," I murmured. He pulled me towards him and kissed my head.

"Great, we can spend more time together."

"Are you sure you're okay playing Romeo?" I asked.

"I'd do anything for you," he murmured, his voice softening as he gazed into my eyes. My heart pounded against my chest.

"Are you guys already rehearsing?" Zev grinned teasingly, which made me redden.

"How come you never mentioned your super hot girlfriend?" Parker smirked.

"I did. You just never listen," Zev said. Parker ignored him and turned towards Adah.

"If you're ever tired of Zev's candy, I know a couple of-"

"Parker," Zev snapped, and Parker raised his hands in innocence.

"Networking. I'm networking," he said.

Mrs. Kelly walked out of the room, turning towards Parker and Zev who flinched under her stern gaze.

"They're letting you boys off the hook for now. We'll have to wait until the third individual gains consciousness to know what happened, and whether or not he'll press charges. I highly doubt he'll take this to court, but I do expect him to make you boys pay his medical bills," she said. "I spoke with the officer and convinced them to let you go home for today."

"Thank you, Mrs. Kelly," Zev said.

"Honestly, what were you boys thinking?" she mumbled, shaking her head. "Freddie told me a lot about you and said you two were smart boys, so why did you beat someone up so badly?"

They didn't answer, shifting uncomfortably under her intimidating gaze. I squeezed my hands and decided to take the blame.

"I-"

"Ryan made fun of my mom," Parker cut me off. "Zev tried to stop me, but he ended up getting involved too."

Mrs. Kelly glared at him, but she let out a small sigh.

"Parker, I've been working with criminals for years. I know when someone is lying," she said, and he flinched. But the lines on Mrs. Kelly's face softened. "You shouldn't throw away your life like this. You have friends and family who care about you. Hurting yourself is the same thing as hurting those around you."

Her words echoed in my mind.

"Now go home, I have another client to meet. Give me a call when you're called for questioning. If any of the officers try to contact you, inform me first."

Parker and Zev nodded, grateful.

"Thank you, Mrs. Kelly."

Chapter 8: Home

Freddie scolded Parker on the way home, but Parker fell asleep. He rested his head on my shoulder, and I got a whiff of his clean, musky scent. His dark hair tickled my nose, and I could feel him slowly losing himself to the drowsiness. His strong arms were crossed over his chest that rose and fell at a steady pace.

When we arrived, Freddie went to his apartment. He said he had an exam to study for. I promised Freddie I'd looked after him. I went to Parker's apartment. He took out a first aid kit. We hadn't spoken a word since we left the police station. I sat down beside him in the living room and helped him clean his injuries.

I wiped the dried blood off of his knuckles, and he winced when I applied the cream on his cuts. When I finished, the sun was already setting.

I looked up at him. The orange light kissed his olive skin, and before I could stop myself, my hand reached out and touched his bruised cheek. His dark brows furrowed, but he didn't pull away. Instead, he put his rough hand over mine and lowered my hand to his lips and kissed the center of my palm. There was something so gentle and sweet about the small gesture. My heart raced inside my chest.

"What are you thinking about?" He asked me, his voice hoarse but quiet.

"You. I'm always thinking about you."

It was the same answer Parker gave me when I asked him the same question. A low chuckle escaped his lips, and he looked at me with pained eyes.

"You're really cruel, dandelion."

I was confused at first, but remembered Mrs. Kelly's words, and understood what Parker meant. When I hurt myself, I hurt more than just myself. I hurt the people around me, especially Parker.

I asked myself countless times, why did I *need* to leave? But the real question I should have asked myself was, why didn't I stay? Before the Big City, I didn't have a reason to stay. I couldn't see a future for myself. It was as if it were psychologically impossible for me to project myself further than the deadline I had given myself. What would happen next? What would become of me afterward? But the answer remained blank.

Until I moved to the Big City, the life I lived wasn't a life. It was a constant struggle for survival. I was trying to live, but I wasn't living, and I became so exhausted from trying that I decided to try harder one last time. And when you tell yourself that it would be your last time, you magically found a boost of energy, like a marathon runner who sprinted before reaching the finish line after dreadful hours of running. You sprinted because finally, you could see the finish line. You told yourself, it's right there, only a few meters away. And after that, you wouldn't have to suffer any more.

When I came to the Big City, I felt as if the finish line only got further. No, it wasn't that the finish line was getting further. *I* was running slower. I met so many wonderful people who helped me understand why humans lived. Despite the dark days, despite the pain, people found reasons to live. Parker, Freddie, Zev, they all suffered, but they kept going. They kept fighting. They kept *living*.
And suddenly, I found myself wanting to continue the long dreadful marathon with them. I didn't want to reach the finish line early by myself. I wanted to run beside my friends and finish the marathon we called Life, together.

"Why are you crying?" Parker asked, pulling me closer towards him to wipe away my tears. I wondered if Parker would ever love anyone the way he loved me. I didn't ask myself out of arrogance, but because I was genuinely worried. Deep down, Parker who shouted and yelled, Parker who swore and fought, Parker who acted tough and strong, he was and would always be Parker, the man who's suffered greatly.

If I left, would he ever love again?

But an even more terrifying question lurked in my mind.

If I left, would Parker live?

"Dandelion," Parker frowned, brushing his thumb over my lid. "What's wrong?"

"If you stop the alcohol, the cigarettes, and the fighting, I'll start eating," I whispered. His eyes widened. He knew what I meant.

If you stop killing yourself, I'll start living.

"You're just saying that," Parker murmured, pulling away from him as if I had slapped him. He was scared I was giving him false hope.

"I mean it," I insisted. "I'll have my ups and downs, and nothing I do will make the Dark Thoughts go away forever, but… I want to try. I want to live with you, Parker. I want to be happy. No, I *am* happy. I want-"

You, I wanted to say. *I want you.*

But my breath caught in my throat and my chest rose and fell unevenly. Parker pulled my head against his shoulder, gently caressing my hair.

"If I had known that all I'd have to do was beat up Ryan to make you stay, I would have done it ages ago," he grumbled, and I let out a shaky laugh.

"Do you mean it, Conan? You'll stay?" He whispered into my hair, his body tensing. I was so used to hearing him call me Dandelion that it almost felt strange hearing him say my real name.

71

I nodded.

"I'll try my best," I said. I wish I could promise him, but I could never make promises. Promises meant forever, and I didn't believe in forever. I believed in honesty.

"You'll stay too, right?" I sniffled. Parker pulled me at arm's length.

"I wasn't planning on leaving. I'm not going anywhere," he said, and I smiled with tears in my eyes.

"We'll get a house."

"A house?" I echoed, confused by the random suggestion. I found out later on that it wasn't as random as I had thought. Parker had thought about moving out with me for a while. He just never told me until now.

"Yeah, a house. A big one," he said. I loved how his eyes brightened when he was excited. "We'll have our names on the mailbox. Parker Anderson and Conan the Dandelion. What do you think?"

I giggled, rubbing away my tears.

"I love it," I said. "But what about Freddie?"

"We'll have a guest room for him," he reassured me, and it made me happy how he had already thought ahead. "We'll have one for Zev too. And we'll get a dog. You're not allergic to them, are you?"

I shook my head.

"But why a dog?"

"Med school is going to keep me busy, and I'll start doing internships soon. I won't be around as much, so I'd feel better if we had a cute little puppy to protect you while I'm gone."

"What will we name it?" I asked. He raised a shoulder.

"Parker junior," he answered, and I burst into laughter. I don't remember the last time I laughed so much.

"Hey, I'm being serious. Don't make fun of our future baby," Parker frowned, poking my ribs which made me giggle harder.

"Parker junior," I chuckled. "It's a nice name. It reminds me of someone I love."

I smiled, pressing my hands against the sides of his face. Parker had the beautiful gift that allowed him to project himself into the future, a gift that I was deprived of. So I was thankful for moments like these in which he'd share his plans and ideas, taking my hand and guiding me down the museum of possibilities. He showed me every painting and artwork, and each one of them was splendid and beautiful.

"We'll have a home, just you and me," he said, looking deeply into my eyes.

"I'd love that," I smiled.

Parker kissed me and my heart pounded against my chest, it almost hurt. I was nervous as if it were our first time kissing. But he placed his hand on the back of my head and reassuringly stroked my hair, and suddenly, the anxiousness melted away.

His familiar lips were warm and soft. He kissed me gently and then as if he were reaching for something more, he pulled me onto his lap. Wanting him closer, I wrapped my arms around his neck to close the gap between us. His hand slipped up my shirt, and electricity zipped through my body when his fingers wandered up to my bareback, but it wasn't me who pulled away first. It was Parker.

"Wait," he mumbled, running a hand through his dark, tousled hair, only turning it into a more beautiful mess. "This is too risky."

"What's too risky?" I asked, breathless. He looked at me with a shy but stern gaze. I'd never seen Parker give this sort of look, and my racing heart couldn't handle it.

"If we keep kissing," he said slowly, his voice smooth and husky. "I don't think I'll be able to stop."

"Then don't stop," I whispered. Parker swallowed, his eyes on my lips.

"Are you sure you want this?" He asked, hesitant.

"I know I do."

His jaw tightened.

"Slap me if I go too far."

"What-"

74

Before I could finish my sentence, Parker pulled me closer, kissing me hard and eager. It was as if a hungry beast had unleashed from deep within him. Freddie told me he was impressed by how long Parker was going without sex since he and I started dating. And I finally understood why.

Before I knew it, our clothes were off and scattered on the floor. His beautiful, muscular torso was ornamented with fresh bruises.

"Does it hurt?" I asked worriedly, running a finger over the bruised near his waist.

"No, not anymore."

He pushed me onto my back, running his hand through my hair as he kissed me. His other hand trailed down my bare chest, and my nipples hardened beneath his fingers. I inhaled sharply at the jolt of tingles that shot down my spine. I opened my mouth and felt the sweep of his tongue explore my mouth, and there was a sudden ache between my thighs.

Parker kissed my cheek and then my neck, licking my collarbone before his lips settled on my nipple. I felt a wince creep up my throat and quickly clasped a hand over my mouth. Parker looked up at me through his thick lashes with his dark, hungry eyes.

"Don't," his husky voice ordered.

"But-"

He lowered my hand from my mouth and flicked his tongue over my hard nipple. I involuntarily let out a moan, and I felt a smile pull up his lips. He held my wrist so I wouldn't cover my mouth and continued to suck on the same area. I felt heat rush down my waist and up my face, and I was embarrassed by the immense pleasure triggered by his movements.

Parker bit my left nipple and I gasped when he teased the round bead against his tongue that sent a million electric sparks zinging throughout my body.

When he pulled away, a line of saliva stretched between my skin and his lips before it snapped. I looked down and saw teeth marks around my nipples that were no longer a soft pink, but a flourished red.

Parker hooked his fingers on the band of my boxers, lowering them down my knees. My erection sprung free and Parker's brows shot up.

"You're already sticky," he said.

"I'm sorry," I stammered. I didn't know what else to say other than apologies.

"No, don't be," he murmured gently, leaning forward and planting a kiss on my cheek. When he did, his strong torso brushed over my lower member, and another quiver of pleasure erupted through me.

"We'll take it slow. I promise," he whispered into my ear, his hot breath making my mind fuzzy. He coated his fingers with saliva but stopped.

"Conan, you're shaking," he frowned, his voice laced with concern.

"I'm sorry, I can't stop it," I said, pressing my forehead against his bare shoulder to hide. "Does it bother you?"

"Nothing about you bothers me. You know that" he said sternly as if it frustrated him that I'd think otherwise. "We don't have to do this if you don't want to."

"No," I blurted, tightening my grip around his neck.

"Dandelion-"

"Please don't make me beg," I whimpered. I felt Parker stiffen, and he let out a small groan.

"Don't say that. It's turning me on even more," he groaned, sounding tormented. "Are you sure you want to keep going?"

I nodded.

"Like I said," Parker grunted. "Slap me hard if you need me to stop."

I winced when he slid a wet finger into me. He moved it rhythmically, going deep each time. He crooked it slightly and it hit a spot that made it impossible not to moan. Parker's mouth returned to mine, and he put in another finger, pushing further into me. My breath became unsteady and the shaking worsened. I could feel him hesitating, but he didn't stop. Two fingers worked inside me. It hurt and felt uncomfortable, but I could handle it.

Unlike uncle Bo, Parker did it slowly and gently, making sure I was well prepared before inserting the real thing in. He reassured me and made sure I felt secure. He was eager, not desperate. He was lustful, but not greedy. Each movement was done with great expertise and care, and I felt safe in Parker's arms. I was scared, but not of him.

Pain jolted through me when Parker put in a third finger, and my nails dug into his shoulder blades. He must have noticed my discomfort and tried to distract me with kisses. His tongue swirled around mine and gently sucked on it, and my mind became a whirr. The slow burn of arousal began to build inside when he pushed deeper in.

I tried to kiss him back but only moans escaped my swollen lips. He pulled his fingers out and my muscles relaxed. Parker reached over and took a condom from the first aid kit. He smiled at me.

"I keep them everywhere," he chuckled, ripping the wrapper with his teeth. But it wasn't the fact that he had a condom in a first aid kit that worried me. It was the intimidating letters "XXL" printed on the package that made me swallow one too many times.

He unbuckled his pants and removed his briefs, and my eyes stretched in shock.

"Parker, you're huge," I gasped.

"Thank you, I try my best," he grinned teasingly. Parker was tall, strong, and big, but I was small and frail with hardly any meat on my bones. If Parker inserted *that* into me, I'd split into two.

"That's never going to fit me," I gulped nervously.

"Trust me, baby, it will."

Parker slipped his erection into the condom, placing the tip of his cock between my legs. I closed my eyes tightly, but when I did, terrible memories flashed through my mind. I remembered how painful it was and how much I hated it. I remembered how it felt so suffocating and repulsive.

The bite mark that Ryan left on my collarbone burned and my chest tightened when I remembered how he forcefully placed his lips there. I wanted to tear my skin off.

"Conan," Parker murmured, pulling me back to reality. My hands were clinging onto his back and I knew my nails were digging into his skin, but I couldn't find myself letting go. I was scared.

"I'm sorry," I apologized again and again. It saddened me how other men had ruined sex for me. A natural process of life that was supposed to give me pleasure was a source of immense pain. This was supposed to be an intimate moment between me and Parker, but ghosts from my past kept invading my thoughts.

My lids were still closed, and tears streaked down the sides of my face.

"You can hold onto me as tightly as you want. It's okay if you leave scratch marks," he said, kissing my lids. "Open your eyes, dandelion. Look at me."

Hesitant at first, I peered up at him, and his eyes were stern but soft. He lowered his head, leaning down to kiss me tenderly.

"Everything will be okay," he promised. "Just take a deep breath and focus on me."

I nodded, focusing my eyes on Parker.

"It's just you and me," he whispered against my mouth, his nose tickling mine.

Just him and I.

The memories slowly faded away and all I could see was Parker. My eyes widened when he slowly entered me. I felt my insides stretch open and threw my head back, wincing in pain.
"It hurts," I cried, but I didn't tell him to stop. He kissed away my tears.

"I know," he whispered, slowly rocking into me. He raised my knees to my chest so he'd slip deeper into me. I inhaled sharply, my breath ragged. I felt like a never-ending train was pushing into me, and my insides felt like they were going to burst.

"You can still slap me," he reminded me, kissing my ear. He sounded as if he was holding himself in check. A shaky laugh escaped my lips, and he rocked at a slow, moderate pace. The pain lessened, and a sense of pleasure replaced it. As his thrusts gained a steady tempo, my thighs tightened around his hips, and I cried out with the wonderful burning it caused.

"Parker," I moaned, holding him tightly. I loved how his body pressed against mine. I loved how there wasn't an inch that separated us. I loved how his big, rough hands caressed me gently and softly, and how the world fell away when his touch stirred my mind. I loved how his dark hair fell over his beautiful forehead, how he smelled of fresh pine and musk, how his body was strong but careful.

I arched my back and moaned at the pleasure and pain caused by his movements. His fingers intertwined with mine and his movements became more rigid. The noises from his throat grew louder as he quickened his pace, thrusting his pelvis against me. Raw grunts and moans filled the silent room,

I felt myself reaching climax and I didn't know how much longer I could hold it back. My eyes flung open and I cried in pleasure when Parker hit the sweet spot over and over again, pounding harder and harder against it. My nails dug into his skin and sparks flew in my mind. I shook uncontrollably as I orgasmed and Parker thrust one last time, throwing his head back with a husky groan when pleasure took over his core. His head then fell against my chest, still shaking. We were breathless, sweaty, and wet.

Parker lied down beside me and I inched closer towards him, resting my head on his chest while he wrapped around me. We were wordless, both lost in our thoughts and emotions.

I closed my eyes, and for the first time in my life, I could see a future unravel inside my mind. The darkness that once plagued every corner was slowly replaced with splashes of color.

I could imagine a big house with a bright red roof and a wide backyard. Parker's name and mine were engraved in the mailbox in front of the fences. A dog was running around, wagging its tail and barking in joy. A field of dandelions displayed in front of us as we walked outside to take a stroll in the neighborhood.

We'd climb trees and read books, eat snacks and play in the lake, and then when we were tired, we'd sit in a field of dandelions. We'd pluck a dandelion and raise it to the sky, closing our eyes to make a wish, and then blow the blossomed seeds away. Parker would sit beside me, and we'd gaze at the sunset, both lost in thoughts. The day would slowly come to an end, but that was okay. The sun would rise again, and a new day would begin, holding more adventures and stories we'd one day look back to and call life.

The thought of a future, *our* future, felt like a dream. It felt surreal, almost like a fairy tale, something that was too good to be true, and yet, we were here, together.

Chapter 9: Parker's Spot

Ryan was still in the hospital with a broken leg. He didn't press any charges, scared that I'd file a report against him for attempted rape. My friends wanted me to do it, but they knew it was a sensitive topic for me. They gave up on trying to persuade me, but I knew it still lingered in their mind. Ryan could no longer play Romeo, and Parker filled in as his substitute. He came to rehearsal after class to practice his lines with me.

"Bid a sick man in sadness make his will: Ah, word urged to one-" Parker paused, narrowing his dark eyes when raising his script to his nose. "What the fuck is this even supposed to mean?"

"It's Modern English from the 16th century," I said.

"It looks like gibberish to me," he grumbled, running a hand through his thick hair.

I frowned and he stiffened, quickly clearing his voice.

"I mean, er, bid a sick man in sadness make his will: Ah, word ill urged to one that is so ill! In sadness, I love a man," he said. We continued going through our scenes and made it to the kiss scene.

"Clark," Parker said, taking my hands in his. I stiffened as my mind flashed to Ryan. "If you love me, I'll be in your heart. If you hate me, I'll be in your mind. Love me or hate me, but don't push me away."

I focused on Parker's eyes.

"Hate," I murmured, feeling myself relax when he pulled me closer to him. "Such a word does not exist when I'm with you."

"Then prove it," he murmured, his voice almost a whisper. I wanted to tell Parker that he needed to speak louder if he wanted the crowd to hear him, but my instincts told me that he didn't want anyone but me to hear him.

"Prove you love me with a kiss," he whispered huskily, and I felt heat flush my cheeks.

"Eep!" someone squealed. We turned towards the group of girls standing in front of the stage, staring at us with their hands pressed together. I blinked blankly, wondering who they were. Parker seemed annoyed by their presence.

"Oh, don't mind us. Please go on," one of them grinned, and the rest nodded eagerly. It made me slightly uncomfortable how widely they were grinning. Parker tightened his jaw and turned back towards me. He opened his mouth to repeat his lines.

"OMG, they're so cute," one of them giggled.

"I can't wait for the real performance," another whispered.

"Eek! They're, like, totally in love," squealed another. Parker twitched, snapping his head towards them.

"Will you keep it down?! We're trying to-"

They climbed onto the stage and gathered around us.

"Oh my god, he's so cute," one of them said, leaning closely into my face. The girls all bobbed their heads in agreement, and I suddenly felt overwhelmed by all the attention. I looked at Parker in panic, but all I could see was a tide of grinning girls. Were they Parker's fans? I knew he had a lot of female friends and admirers, but I didn't think they'd come into the theatre room and watch us rehearse. Then again, we have been getting a lot of girls coming here to watch our rehearsals since Parker took the lead role.

"He's so small. Look at his small hands!"

I looked down at my fingers and wiggled them. *Small hands? I guess they're a lot smaller than Parker's, but still...*

"Ahhh, he's so cute," one of them wailed.

"He looks like my little brother but ten times cuter," another said.

"He's a baby. I just want to pinch his cheeks and hug him!" another said. My eyes widened at the last part. Parker grabbed my hand and pulled me out of the circle of girls, protectively standing in front of me.

"Absolutely not," he snapped harshly.

"That's not fair. Why are you hogging him?" one of them frowned.

"Parker, you never told us you had such an adorable friend," one of them sulked.

"Yeah," another agreed. "Why are you hiding your friend?"

Parker's jaw ticked.

"He's not my friend! He's my boyfriend. Now, will you back the fuck off? You're scaring him," he said, which caused many heads to turn our way. He bit his lower lip, realizing the mistake he made. The girls' jaws dropped to the ground, their eyes as wide as saucepans.

"OMG, YOU TWO ARE DATING?!" one of them screamed. Within seconds, Parker and I were surrounded by a group of people throwing questions at us. *How long have you been dating? Have you two kissed yet? How did you two meet? Who made the first move?*

I watched as Parker tried to answer them, but he looked flustered. I found myself giggling when I saw his cheeks turn red. I've never seen Parker look so nervous. For some reason, his fangirls were crazy about us and enjoyed seeing us together. But rather than their attention, I enjoyed standing beside Parker and seeing this new side of him.

I knew it was impossible to know everything about a person. There would always be secrets and thoughts he'd keep to himself. It wasn't a question of secrecy, but privacy. We all needed to keep a small part of us to ourselves. But I wanted to see as many sides of Parker as I could, as many as he'd let me.

I gently squeezed his hand to let him know I was here for him. Despite all the chaos, he squeezed back.

***

The backstage was bustling. Students were rushing to-and-fro, hurrying to put on their clothes and accessories. Some were going through their lines while others put on their make-up. Everyone was extremely stressed as the theatre room slowly filled with people. We've been practicing for months, and everyone was nervous. Today was the big day. I peeked through the red curtains and stiffened when I saw people flowing through the entrance, but a smile pulled across my face when I saw Zev, Freddie, and Adah sitting in the front row. Where was Freddie's boyfriend? Freddie told me he'd come, but the seat on his left was empty.

Zev's eyes met mine and he grinned widely, waving at me excitedly. I smiled back, waving. I wanted to get off the stage and talk to my friends, but someone called my name.

"Conan!" the theatre teacher called. I closed the curtains and turned towards her. She looked frantic as if she was seconds away from having a panic attack.

"Good evening, Mrs. Lizzo," I said. "How are you?"

"I'm seconds away from having a mental breakdown."

"Oh, I see. Would you like some candy?" I asked. Zev gave me a handful of candy this morning for good luck.

"Where is Parker?" she demanded, and I blinked blankly.

"I don't know."

Mrs. Lizzo clutched her chest, taking loud, deep breaths.

"We can't find him. He won't answer his phone, and no one has seen him around," she said. "He's the main lead! The show can't start without him!"

I frowned. Parker wasn't someone to break promises. He kissed my forehead this morning and said he'd be here.

"You have to help us find him. Please, Conan," Mrs. Lizzo begged. I nodded calmly.

"Okay," I said. "I think I might know where he is."

Mrs. Lizzo embraced me, squeezing me tightly against her squishy chest before finally releasing me.

"You're a lifesaver," she said.

I left the school and rushed out the back door. A cold winter breeze kissed my cheeks when I stepped outside. The world was grey and covered in white. It was snowing. Parker was leaning against a metal ramp, his hands stuffed into his coat. He brought his cigarette to his lips, tilting his head back and letting out a puff of smoke that slowly vanished above him. His dark eyes stared at the empty sky, and he seemed lost in his thoughts.

There it was again, that strange sense of loneliness that never seemed to leave his side. I felt a pinch of pain when I looked at him. Since the first day I'd met him, there'd always been something melancholic about Parker.

I walked up to him and the sound of snow crunching beneath my feet caught his attention. He looked at me, his eyes now focused, and he smiled.

"Hey, Dandelion. Caught me red-handed."

"How many?" I whispered. Cigarettes and bottles were another way of measuring his level of pain.

He paused, hesitated, then said, "Five."

He caught the frown on my face.

"Sorry, I know we agreed on three," he mumbled.

"It's okay. I know you smoke when something is on your mind," I said, standing beside him and looking up at the sky. What was he gazing so intently at? There was nothing but a gray haze. "Why are you out here? It's cold."

"I needed some time to think," he answered vaguely, flicking the ashes from the tip of his cigarette. He didn't bring it to his lips anymore and let it burn between his fingers. His other hand fidgeted as if they were aching to reach for a bottle of vodka.

"Conan, why do you write in your journal?" he asked suddenly.

"My journal?"

"You keep a journal under your pillow, and you write in it every night."

"I write so I don't forget the memories I make no matter where I am in the world. Our lives are limited, and death is constant. We live knowing we'll die, which is why I believe we were born to create. We have art and literature to crystallize our existence. It leaves a trace of what has passed, and it works as a loophole to cheat Death. It renders us eternal, infinite. Even if we no longer exist, our words carry our legacies."

Parker's jaw tightened. "You sound like someone who's planning on leaving. You're not leaving, are you?"

"I said I wouldn't go anywhere, remember?" I murmured, wondering why he looked so anxious.

Parker didn't answer. Something must be bothering him.

"I used to write for myself," I said, hoping to reassure him.

"And now?"

"I write for you."

His eyebrows pulled together.

"What do you mean?"

"You'll understand one day," I murmured. Before he could any me any more questions, I spoke first. "Are you okay?"

"Yeah, I'm fine."

I didn't believe him, so I tried again.

"Are you okay?" I asked.

There was a long pause, and then a short chuckle.

"Would you think I'm a jerk if I said I was thinking about Eden?" he asked, a trace of guilt ricocheting in his voice. I didn't answer. "I was looking at the audience and I saw all these people sitting down, and I couldn't help but wish he was amongst them. It's stupid, I know. How can a dead person come back to life? But that didn't stop me from hoping."

He tilted his head and stared back at the sky as if searching for something. *Someone.*

"I want to sit down and talk to him," Parker said, swallowing hard. "I want to tell him how much I miss him, and that even though he's no longer here, I still look for him, constantly, unconditionally. And that the world is painfully lonely without him, and that it'll never be the same no matter what I do, and how sad I am to see the world changing without him, that I'm changing without him. I want to tell him I met a wonderful boyfriend named Conan, that I love him more than he loves philosophy, that I feel guilty for falling in love again, and that I'm sorry for moving on but not entirely," he paused, taking in a shaky breath. "I guess what I'm trying to say is, there's so much I want to tell him but can't."

When I looked at Parker who fought so hard to speak, fought so hard to hold back his tears. Death wasn't about the dead. Death was about Life. It was about those who lived and had to move forward; the living who, like a wounded soldier in an endless battlefield, had to carry on surviving; the living who strapped a rope over their shoulder dragging a ghost behind them. Not a corpse, but a phantom. Because when you looked over your shoulder, there was nothing attached to the other side of the rope. What was there to look at? The dead had been freed from the world and its burdens. What you dragged wasn't physical, but something bleak and imperceptible. You couldn't get rid of it because how did one get rid of something that didn't exist? That *no longer* existed? And so, you looked ahead and clung onto life with a weight in your heart that would never seize to vanish, climbing forward.

"I'm forgetting someone I can't forget. It's like he's dead but not entirely. Where does that leave me?" he rasped, and I could hear a slight tremor in his husky voice. "I'm caught between being happy and him. I wish he'd set me free. I wish someone would set me free."

He stared at nothing.

"Would you believe me if I said I'm in so much pain, I could die?"

My eyes widened and my hand instinctively reached out for his. He flinched and turned towards me as if my touch snapped him out of his trance.

"Don't say that," I whispered. I couldn't imagine my life without Parker. I could imagine life, but not *a* life. "Please, don't say that."

He blinked and he laughed sheepishly.

"Right, I'm sorry. My stupid mouth just doesn't know when to shut up," he said, pulling me closer and kissing my forehead. "Hey, don't cry. I'm here, aren't I?"

He lowered his head to meet my eye-level.

"The reason why I'm standing out here in the cold like an idiot is that there are over three hundred people in the theatre room waiting for us to play a gay version of Romeo and Juliet, and it's making me nervous," he whispered as if it was a secret between him and I. "Honestly, I feel like I'm going to shit my pants. I even brought meds for explosive diarrhea just in case."

His words caught me by surprise, and I found myself laughing.

"Hey, I'm serious!" He said defensively. "You don't believe me?"

He took out a box of pills for diarrhea and I burst into giggles. Parker truly was great at changing subjects. He slipped the box into his pocket, looking at me with a worried smile.

"Aren't you nervous?" he asked quietly.

"No."

"Gee, thanks, that makes me feel so much better."

"I think I'm not nervous because," I paused, feeling my heart beat against my rib cage. It was so quiet; I could almost hear my pulse racing. "Because my friends are here. The people I love are here. And," I felt shy but mustered up to courage to meet his gaze, his wonderful dark eyes brighter than the grey sky. "*You're* here. You're-"

"Here and here," he whispered, repeating the same gestures I made months ago, gently pressing his fingers against my chest, touching his spot. Parker's spot.

I nodded.

"Here and here," I echoed, warmth spreading through my body despite the wintry breeze. "So there's nothing to worry about. That's how I know I'm okay."

Before I could register what happened, Parker's lips pressed against mine. He tasted like cigarettes. My mouth widened and he slipped his tongue in, cupping my face in his hands as he deepened the kiss. I winced when he bit my lower lip, pulling it slightly before finally releasing it. His beautiful forehead pressed against mine, the warmth of his hands spreading through my entire body.

"Fuck," he rasped, tightly closing his eyes as if it was torturing him not to kiss me again. "If we didn't have to go on stage in ten minutes, I'd take your clothes off in a heartbeat."

He tugged at my clothes.

"Fuck," he grumbled again, sounding even more disappointed. "This sucks."

I put my hands over his and smiled.

"We'll have time after the play. Let's do our best tonight."

Parker looked at me and nodded. I was right. He looked more handsome when he smiled.

Chapter 10: Together

The play was a major success. When we gathered to the front, holding hands and bowing down, the audience clapped loudly and cheered. Zev was screaming our names, and I giggled as we bowed once more. The curtains fell, and I let out a small sigh of relief. I looked up at Parker, who smiled back. Mrs. Lizzo dashed towards us with wide arms. Parker pulled me back and took the embrace for my stead.

"You two were amazing!" Mrs. Lizzo exclaimed, squeezing the oxygen out of Parker's lungs. She released Parker. "You have to join our next play. We're thinking of doing a re-adaptation of Hamlet."

Mrs. Lizzo tried to persuade me and Parker to try out for the roles, but we both knew this 'Romeo, oh Romeo' would be our first and last play. My eyes brightened when

I saw two familiar faces. I bolted towards Zev and hugged him tightly.

"For you," Zev beamed, handing me a bouquet. It was so big, it blocked my entire view.

"Thank you, Zev!" I said, even though I could see him. He chuckled, taking the bouquet.

"We'll ask Parker to hold it," he winked. Freddie hugged me too.

"You were amazing," he said, his eyes pink from tears. But when he pulled away, I noticed a bruise near his wrist. I frowned.

"Where did you get that?" I asked worriedly, and he quickly pulled down his sleeves.

"Just a small accident," he quickly said, but something didn't feel right. I was about to say something, but Parker arrived.

"Let's get outta here before Mrs. Lizzo comes," he whispered, ushering us towards the exit. "I'm starving. Who's buying dinner?"

Zev and Freddie agreed to treat us out. We went to 'Hot Cakes' which was a restaurant that had a variety of pancakes. You could have pancakes for breakfast, lunch, and dinner. It was one of our favorite places to eat. Who didn't love having breakfast for dinner? But as happy and relieved as I was to have finished the play, the bruise on Freddie's wrist bothered me.

***

I went to take out the trash but met Freddie on the way down. He was wearing sunglasses, but the sky was grey.

"Good afternoon, Freddie," I waved. He seemed startled when he saw me, but quickly smiled.

"Hey, Conan." There was a slight tremor in his voice.

"How are you?"

"Oh, I'm good. Thanks." He quickly scurried down the stairs as if he was in a hurry, but he slipped on the last step and fell. I went down and picked up the sunglasses that fell off his face and handed them to him. My eyes widened when I saw his swollen eye. There was a bruise around it.

"Freddie, what happened?" I asked. Freddie snatched the sunglasses out of my hand and put them back on to hide his injury.

"It's nothing," he stammered. He brushed past me.

"Was it your boyfriend?" I asked. Freddie froze stiff, giving away the answer, and my chest tightened with panic. Many questions popped in my head, and I had to carefully choose the most essential ones. "Did he hurt you anywhere else? How long has this been happening?"

"Don't tell Parker and Zev," he whispered, his back turned towards me.

"You have to tell the police about this. They-"

"No, I don't. It's fine, I have everything handled," he blurted harshly, and I felt an overwhelming feeling take over me. I thought it was fear at first, but I had feared my entire life and knew this wasn't it. No, I was angry.

"Freddie, you have to tell someone," I insisted. Freddie looked surprised by the tone of my voice, as was I.

"*I* have to tell someone?" he scoffed, his tone bitter and cold. "Don't tell me to do something you aren't capable of doing."

Freddie stormed away before I could stop him. He avoided me after that day. We didn't go to university together and took separate cars. Whenever I waved and smiled at him, he'd return a tiny smile before scurrying away. Zev invited us for brunch at 'Hot Cakes' Sunday afternoon. We sat at our usual booth and ate our pancakes. Zev was the only one talking, trying his best to lighten up the mood. He sighed.

"What kind of brunch is this? I buy you guys food and you just sit here and sulk?" he grumbled. "Why aren't you talking to each other?"

Freddie glanced at me with an anxious look in his eyes. Was he scared I'd tell Zev and Parker about his abusive boyfriend? I stared at the menu even though we had already ordered. As much as I wanted to tell them, it was Freddie's secret. I was being a terrible person by not telling them, but I was being a loyal friend by keeping my mouth shut. Loyal didn't mean good, but it meant I was still Freddie's friend. I tried to put myself in his shoes. I would have never forgiven Freddie if he had told the police when Ryan came to my place, which only made me feel worse.

We went back to Zev's car, and he drove us home. Our problems were still unresolved.

"Can we build a snowman?" I asked when we arrived at our building.

"A snowman?" Zev inquired.

"Winter is almost over, and the snow is melting. I've always wanted to build a snowman with my friends."

Zev didn't give Freddie a chance to answer. "Let's do it."

He parked his car, and we went to the small park in front of our apartment building. The green grass was covered in a layer of untouched snow. I crouched down and pressed a lump of snow between my mittens before rolling it forward. When the snowball got too big for me to roll, Freddie came and helped. We silently worked on our snowman together. We found two twigs to use as his arms and pebbles for his nose and eyes. I snapped a picture of Freddie and Zev and sent it to Parker.

Me: *Hello, Parker, it's Conan. I'm building a snowman with Freddie and Zev. Would you like to join us?*

Parker: *No.*

Me: *Okay! We're downstairs in front of the apartment if you ever change your mind.*

Me: *Freddie is sad.*

Parker: *Why? What happened?*

I didn't know how to answer his question, so I tucked my phone into my pocket and joined my friends. Five minutes later, Parker came out of the building. He stared at our snowman with a scowl.

"That is the ugliest thing I've seen in my life, and that's saying a lot."

He didn't say anything else and helped us finish the snowman. Parker found the prettiest pebbles and pressed them into the snow in a horizontal line. It looked like buttons. When we were done, we stepped back and admired our creation.

"It looks like a mutant alien," Parker said flatly.

"What should we name it?" Zev smiled.

"E.T."

"I think we should name it Martin," Freddie said. We all looked towards him in surprise.

"Martin, as in your boyfriend?" Parker asked.

"Yeah."

Silence.

"Alright, we'll name him Martin," Zev said, breaking the silence. He grabbed Martin's twig arms and broke it on his knee. "Fuck you, Martin."

Parker grabbed his other twig arm and crushed it under his foot.

"I never liked you anyway," Parker shrugged. Parker and Zev looked at me. Was it my turn?

I went up to Martin and kicked him, but my foot got stuck in his belly.

"You're not a good person, Martin," I said, but when I pulled my boot out, the snowman's head rolled off and smashed into a gazillion pieces. I blinked, turning toward my friends.

"I think I killed Martin," I frowned.

They all stared at me and burst into laughter.

"I love you so much, Conan. Don't ever change," Zev said, putting his arm over my shoulder. We laughed until we noticed Freddie crying.

"Aw, baby, don't cry," Zev frowned. "He wasn't worth it anyway."

"If you're going to be gay, the least you can do is have better taste in men," Parker snorted. Freddie flicked him a finger and Parker rolled his eyes, pulling him in and hugging him.

"I told you he was rich trash," he grumbled, and Freddie laughed and cried. Parker and Zev didn't ask any more questions concerning Martin. They didn't ask why Freddie cried or what had happened. They simply let him feel all the emotions he needed to feel. When I asked Zev why, he said, 'He'll talk when he's ready.'

But what if Freddie was never ready? What if he kept hiding his bruises and injuries? The thought of Freddie suffering alone terrified me. When everyone went home, I asked Freddie if we could talk alone.

"Freddie?" I said. "I'm sorry."

Tears pricked his eyes, but he smiled sadly. "I'm sorry too. I shouldn't have said such nasty things last week."

I shook my head.

"If I file a report, will you file one too?"

Freddie blinked in surprise. "What?"

"I'll tell the police and take it to court. I'll most likely lose the trial since there are no witnesses or proof of what happened, but I'll do it," I said.

The bite mark on my collarbone was the only proof I had, but so much time had passed that it had faded. There was nothing I could show the police to prove what happened, and Ryan would most likely deny my accusations. My words would be nothing but hollow ones. It was too late for me, but that didn't matter. I didn't want revenge, nor did I want to punish Ryan. What I wanted was to give

Freddie the courage to do the same. It wasn't too late for him.

"Why?" Freddie whispered.

"Because I love you," was all I said, but I said those simple words with all my heart.

Freddie looked at me and tears streaked down his cheeks. He hugged me tightly, sobbing.

"Okay," he whispered, his voice trembling. "We'll do it together."

I smiled, hugging him back.

"Together."

Chapter 11: The Trial

I went to Freddie's mother's office to discuss the report I filed against Ryan. I couldn't verbally tell her what happened. My thoughts would jumble up, my lungs would tighten, and I'd simply sit there focusing on how to breathe than anything else. She told me it was fine and gave me a cup of water. She was such a nice lady.

"How about you write what happened instead? It might be easier for you," she suggested softly.

"May I please borrow a pen and paper? I didn't bring anything with me," I said.

"Of course."

She handed me the material and left the room so I wouldn't feel uncomfortable. I wanted to call Parker to help ease the pain in my chest, but I had to stop relying on him. I needed to learn how to stand on my own. I took in a deep breath and began writing. Once I was done, Freddie's mom returned and read what I wrote. Her face darkened as her eyes scanned the lines.

"I'm so sorry this happened," she said, finally looking up. I shifted in my seat and simply nodded. "I believe you, Conan, I really do. But the tricky thing about the law is that everything needs to be objective. Do you have any proof that would be able to prove Ryan guilty? Security cameras, videos, pictures, a vocal testimony…?"

"I had a bruise on my shoulder, but it's healed now," I answered, and she frowned.

"Then our only hope is that your case is resolved through a plea bargain, but I highly doubt Ryan will admit to his crimes."

"What's a plea bargain?" I asked.

"It's an agreement between the prosecutor and perpetrator's representative. Ryan would have to agree to plead guilty on his own accord in return for a reduction in penalty," she explained. "We can take this to court, but even if you press charges, I don't think you'll win."

"It's okay if I don't win," I said, and she raised an arched eyebrow. "I'm doing this for my best friend."

"You want to take this to court even if you lose the prosecution?" she asked quizzically. I smiled, although I didn't know why I was smiling.

"Yes."

We continued discussing the prosecution process, and for the next two weeks, I went to her office almost every day. When Freddie saw that I had kept my word, he also filed a report. Unlike me, Freddie had proof. He went to the hospital and had a medical checkup, showing the doctors his bruises and injuries. On the day of my prosecution, I was told to wear a suit. I went downstairs where Parker waited for me. He smiled when he saw me.

"Hey, dandelion," he murmured, pulling me towards him and kissing my head. "You look amazing."

"Thank you," I said, feeling warmth spread through my cheeks as I looked into his dark eyes.

"Are you ready?" He seemed more nervous than me. And for the first time in a while, I felt ready.

"I'll be fine," I promised. Parker bit his lower lip but nodded. He drove us to court. Parker and Zev weren't allowed to attend the prosecution, but they promised to wait outside the building for me. Freddie couldn't attend either because he had to meet his lawyer. When we arrived at the building, Parker looked at me.

"I hope you win," he whispered, even though we both knew that the odds were against me. I thought it was beautiful and sad how humans pocketed hope. Even during the darkest days, they'd keep a small light in their pockets, wishing fate would miraculously play in their favor. I was about to leave, but Parker caught my arm and kissed me on the lips. They were warm and soft. He pulled away, closed his eyes, and took in a deep breath.

"Are you okay?" I asked.

"Yes, I'm fine." But he wouldn't let me go.

"I'll be okay," I reassured him.

"Mhm, I know," but he seemed worried. I smiled, cupping his jaw in my small hands. He opened his eyes, his thick lashes revealing his dark eyes.

"Don't worry about me," I whispered, our foreheads pressed together.

"Okay," he replied with worry. I laughed, kissing his lips. I went in for a quick peck, but Parker had a different idea. He ran his hand through my hair, placing his hand on the back of my neck to pull me closer. And despite the gloomy weather, the world brightened. I let my fingers slide down his sharp, angular face while he pressed his lips harder against mine, opening my mouth with his, kissing me endlessly. My body burned with heat, and my lungs begged for oxygen, and so I pulled away despite my reluctance. Parker let out a discontent growl, kissing down my face, then the base of my throat, before letting his face fall on my shoulder. I could hear his quick, raspy breaths match mine. His large hand was placed dangerously close to my inner thigh.

I swallowed hard, trying to chase away the fuzziness.

"I have to go," I whispered.

"I know, but…" his voice trailed. He stopped, then sighed, looking up at me with defeated eyes. "I know."

"I'll be okay," I said.

"But I won't."

He pulled away, and my body immediately yearned for his warmth. Parker put his hands on the steering wheel and tightened his grip as if he was scared his hands would wander elsewhere if he didn't hold something.

"I'll wait for you here," he said, and a curve pulled on the corner of his lips as he tilted his head in such an adorable way, my heart skipped a beat. "Go kick ass."

I picked up my bag and left his car, entering the large building. Freddie's Mom was waiting for me at the entrance.

"What took you so long?" she asked sternly.

"I'm sorry, I was kissing my boyfriend," I frowned, feeling guilty for making her wait. She blinked, then sighed.

"You are a very honest man. Perhaps too honest," she murmured, but her voice was soft. "Please fix your hair. We don't want the judge to know you've had a make-out session with your boyfriend before you arrived."

I nodded, quickly patting my hair down. We went to the courtroom. There were a few people in the audience, but none I knew. Sitting on the front left was Ryan. My body froze stiff when I saw him. He had stitches on the side of his face, and there were a pair of crutches set beside him. When his gaze met mine, fear flashed through his eyes. But he wasn't scared of me. He was scared of Parker and Zev who beat him up. He looked away. I went to the solicitor box on the right, preparing my papers with

Freddie's Mom, and the session began. We were asked to stand up.

"Conan Sonder, you have asked to press charges against Ryan Llian for sexual harassment," the judge said, his wise, grey eyes piercing into me. It took me a few seconds to find my voice.

"Yes, Your Honor," I replied.

"Do you swear to tell the truth, and nothing but the truth?"

"I do solemnly, sincerely, and truly declare and affirm that the evidence I shall give shall be the truth, the whole truth and nothing but the truth."

He nodded. "You wrote that Mr. Llian had tried to force himself upon you in your domicile?"

"Yes, Your Honor."

"Did he have your consent?"

"No, Your Honor."

"Did you ask Mr. Llian to stop?"

"Yes, Your Honor."

"Do you have any evidence that may prove this?"

"No more than my words, Your Honor."

He turned towards Ryan Llian.

"Ryan Llian, you are accused of sexually harassing Mr. Sonder. Do you swear to tell the truth, and nothing but the truth?"

"I do solemnly, sincerely, and truly declare and affirm that the evidence I shall give shall be the truth, the whole truth and nothing but the truth," he said solemnly.

"Have you conducted inappropriate behavior towards Mr. Sonder without his consent?"

Everyone stared at Ryan, whose jaw tightened. His sickeningly blue eyes locked with my gaze.

"No, Your Honor," he said. And I remembered how great of an actor Ryan was. The judge continued volleying questions, and Ryan's lawyer defended his case, insisting on the fact that I had no solid evidence to prove Ryan's crimes. His lawyer accused me of being obsessed with him after having met him at our university's theatre room, and that I was only doing this to get his attention. He claimed that I was a stalker, which was when Mrs. Kelly intervened and said that he was making false accusations.

"After the debate and discussion, I will now pass sentence the verdict that Ryan Llian is found not guilty," he said. "Court adjourned."

He used his gavel to end the process. The room filled with whispers and murmurs as they stood up from their seats, getting ready to leave. Mrs. Kelly gently squeezed my arm.

"I'm sorry, Conan," she whispered.

"Thank you for everything," I replied with a small smile.

And despite losing the trial, I was proud of myself. It was the first time I had taken action against someone who had done something wrong, and not only that, but I was able to give strength to Freddie who would hopefully find the justice he deserved.

We left the courtroom, and my eyes widened. Freddie stood across the hall from me, wearing a suit. His brilliant orange hair shined brightly, and the freckles on his face seemed particularly visible today. His gaze met mine, searching for the answer given by the judge. I felt a lump in my throat, squeezing my hands at my sides. I didn't want to disappoint Freddie. He saw the look on my face and sadness crossed his eyes, but then he smiled.

He walked up to me and wrapped his arms tightly around me. My head tilted slightly back, and I stared at the ceiling, feeling his body quiver against mine. I gently patted his back, hoping the small gesture was enough to hold him together.

"I'm so proud of you, Conan," he rasped, and tears pricked my eyes. He broke into sobs, apologizing and thanking me, and I held onto him. I felt a prickle of sadness and happiness and thought today was a strange victory.

***

A few weeks later, Freddie went to the courtroom for his trial. He sacrificed his dignity, revealing the horrors he went through during the past few months in front of a judge and an unknown audience, also revealing his sexuality, which wasn't an easy task. But he had collected enough evidence to win his trial. Martin was accused of sexual and physical abuse and was sentenced to three years in prison. When Freddie walked out of the courtroom with tears in his eyes and a quivering smile on his face, I thought to myself, life was beautiful and tragic.

Justice didn't always prevail, but that didn't mean life was doomed to be miserable. Not everything in life was fair, but it compensated for the misfortunate events in different ways. Even if I had lost my trial, Freddie won his. I found my happiness in Freddie's victory.

Chapter 12: Thirsty

Dear,

There comes a time in life when the world changes. The way you perceive it is different. The world you saw as a child and the one you see growing up are different. The world itself didn't change, but your perception does.

My life has changed after meetingmy friends. Life has its ups and downs, but it is no longer a constant plummet downwards. I know my friends will be by my side during my darkest and brightest days. I know Parker will be by my side.

Yours Truly

***

It was April. Spring began to bloom, and the winter snow melted away. The weather was warm, so Zev invited us to his villa for Easter down in the Southern region. It was warmer than the Big City and less polluted.

Parker, Freddie, Zev, Adah, and I packed our things for the weekend. It was still cold to swim in the lake, but Parker and Zev stripped their clothes off and sprinted to the lake as soon as we arrived.

Zev and Parker caught the attention of bystanders, particularly women. Zev's skin was a beautiful crisp gold. His muscles in his torso were sharp and prominent, and he had a natural grin that would make anyone's heart flutter. Parker stood out too much. He pushed back his dark hair, revealing his beautiful forehead, and his smooth, olive skin glistened under the sun. Zev and Parker played around like kids, splashing each other and giggling, but the women nearby perceived them as men.

"Come on, you guys should join us!" Zev called. Freddie and I shared a look and smiled.

"I'll finish unpacking. You guys go ahead," Adah said.

"Don't you want to swim with us?" Freddie asked.

"It's too cold," she chuckled. "Besides, who else is going to take care of you guys when the four of you catch a cold?"

Freddie and I laughed sheepishly, but we changed into our swimsuits and headed to the lake. Parker swam towards me, approaching me like an alligator. He bumped his nose against my waist, wrapping his strong arms around me. His body felt warm underneath the water. He kissed my waist with his soft lips.

"What are you doing?" I laughed. He emerged from the water and had to tilt my head back to meet his gaze.

"Kissing you, what else?"

He leaned in to kiss me, but a violent tide splashed against us. Our eyes darted towards Zev, who had a grin too wide for his face. Freddie was sitting on his shoulders, smiling as well.

"Oh, it's on," Parker smirked, wiping the water that dripped from his chin. He disappeared under the water and bubbles popped on the surface. My eyes widened when I felt his head squeezed between my thighs. He held onto my legs and stood up below me. I yelped, holding onto his head so I wouldn't fall. He stood up, and I was sitting on his shoulders.

Before I knew what was happening, he charged towards Zev. Freddie tried to push me off of Parker, who held tightly onto my legs.

"Fight back, dandelion," Parker urged. But I didn't want to hurt Freddie. Parker bent his knees, taking in a mouthful of water and shooting it at Freddie, who screamed in horror.

"Dude, that's disgusting!" Freddie cried. He let his guard down, and I pushed him back. He yelped, crashing into the waters with a loud splash. Parker cackled with laughter, raising his hand at me. I stared at his palm.

"You're supposed to hit my hand," Parker said. I opened my hand and hit his hand. He grinned widely, and my heart fluttered. It was the first time I had ever given a high five.

"I demand a rematch!" Freddie said, after scrubbing his face.

"Don't be a sore loser, Chucky," Parker snorted haughtily, giving him a gentle splash. Freddie narrowed his eyes and chased me and Parker. We played in the lake for the rest of the afternoon. Parker went to tan in the sun while Zev and Freddie went back to the house. I swam a little more before getting out of the water. Parker was stretched on a tanning bed. He was wearing sunglasses, so I couldn't see his eyes, but his glistening body was very much visible.

His body was muscular without being bulky, and his skin was a beautiful olive shade. Pearls of water trickled down his smooth skin, and his raven-black hair looked like the darkest shade of purple under the sun. My eyes wandered to his legs. I couldn't stop glancing down. It was as if his body was a new form of addiction to my eyes, leaving me desperate to see past the fabric of his swim shorts. Seeing another man's body used to disgust me. Now it left me craving for more. I tore my eyes away before I got any ideas.

"Did you finish swimming?" Parker asked, peering at me over his dark shades. I nodded. My eyes stopped at his crotch again and my imagination was sent spiraling. Flustered, I looked away.

"Are you okay?" he asked, picking up a towel. When I crouched down, he put it over my head and dried my hair.

"Yes," I said. "I'm going to head to the house."

"Do you mind putting some sunscreen on my back for me?" he asked. When I didn't answer immediately, he said, "It's fine if you can't."

He must have thought that I wasn't comfortable touching him.

"I can." The words came out before I could think them through, and Parker pursed his lips.

"Are you sure?"

"No." But I picked up the bottle of sunscreen. I squeezed the thick liquid into my hand and Parker rolled onto his stomach. I knew he was looking at me intently through his tinted glasses. I slowly rubbed the yellowish cream between my palms. It felt sticky.

I placed my hands on his strong shoulder. His body was wet but warm, and his skin was smooth. I slowly started to rub down his back, letting my fingers feel every tense muscle near his shoulder blades. My breath quicker and heat rushed to my waist, and I felt like I was at that early teenage phase during puberty when you couldn't control what happened beneath your briefs.

"Can you put some on my legs too?" Parker asked. And so I did, starting from his ankle and up to his strong thighs. My legs were so thin and frail compared to his. Parker and Zev loved going to the gym together. His body felt nice, but I bit my lower lip when I felt my Southern region twitch. I quickly stood up.

"Where are you going?" I heard Parker call after me, but my mind was too busy trying to focus on finding a place to hide. I found a small shed and walked into it. My hands were still covered in sunscreen, and Parker's warmth still lingered on my skin.

I looked down and stiffened. The middle of my swimsuit was formed into the shape of a tent, and heat rushed up to my neck. Someone knocked at the door.

"Conan?" Parker called.

"Yes, I'm here," I replied, but I wish I wasn't. I tried to get it down, but I've never experienced a situation of sudden arousal. I used to think I was impotent. And now that it was happening, I didn't know what to do. I pressed my palm against it, but it only made it bigger.

Parker tried to open the door, but I closed it back shut.

"Why are you hiding in a shed?" He asked.

"An unfortunate incident happened, and I'm trying to fix it," I explained.

"Unfortunate incident? Are you hurt?" His voice was thick with worry. I felt ashamed to tell him I had an erection, so I tried to find a different way to tell him.

"It's a pleasurable kind of hurt," I said.

Silence. Did Parker leave?

"From touching me?" He asked.

"I will fix the problem if you give me a few minutes to find a solution," I said, looking around to see if there was anything useful in the shed. There was a hammer, a rake, and a toolbox, but nothing that could help me.

"Open the door," Parker said softly.

"The problem hasn't been fixed," I informed him, still searching.

"I'll help you fix it."

My spine stiffened, and the thought of letting Parker touch me worsened the situation. I adjusted my wet swimsuit, trying to give myself more space down below.

"No, I can fix it," I tried to reassure him.

"It'll be quicker with my help."

Before I could protest, he said, "I want to help."

I blinked in surprise.

"Can I come in?" He asked. When he opened the door, I didn't close it shut, and Parker's strong, lean body stood in front of me. I put my hands in front of my waist, staring at my wrinkly toes.

"Good afternoon, Parker," I said.

"Why won't you look at me?"

"I'm embarrassed."

"Getting an erection is a natural phenomenon," he chuckled coolly, which made me feel a little less ashamed. "But I didn't think you were such a naughty boy."

I knew he was teasing me, but my ears burned with heat.

"I can help if you let me," he murmured, his voice low and husky, but there was nothing oppressive in his tone. I gulped, pressing my lips together. My throat felt too tight to speak, so I simply nodded. I wondered if Parker would use a hammer to fix my lower member. Would it be painful?

My eyes widened when Parker crouched down and got on his knees. Before I could stop him, he pulled my trunks down and my erection sprung free. I held back a gasp when his mouth embraced the tip.

"W-Wait, Parker, we can't do it here," I whimpered, my hands getting lost in his hair as I tried to push his head back. He looked up at me through his dark lashes. My breath hitched at his piercing gaze, and the strength in my arms weakened.

I bit my tongue when Parker pushed my cock deeper into his mouth. When he pulled back, adding pressure by sucking in his cheeks, my knees shook uncontrollably.

"You like that, don't you?" Parker smirked, his red lips pressed against my lower member. His hot breath sent shivers down my spine. "Or do you want me to stop?"

I shook my head frantically, and a husky laugh escaped his throat. I fought back the urge to kiss him. He closed his lips around the sensitive head and sucked, swirling his tongue against my slit. My small hands tightened in his ravenous, wet hair, and I tried not to make any noises. But it was impossible not to. Parker was experienced. I failed to hold back my moan when I felt my tip go deeper into his mouth. My back arched and my knees buckled. He sucked in his cheeks and quickened his pace.

"Parker, wait!" I begged, but it was too late. I let out a strained cry when I came into his mouth, and my entire body shook with pleasure. When the world refocused, my eyes widened when I realized what I had done, and I quickly cupped my hands below his chin.

"You can spit in my hands," I said desperately, panting unevenly. I stiffened when Parker swallowed. He used the pad of his thumb to wipe the excess liquid off his lips, and my heart stopped when he sucked it clean.

"You taste sweet," he said casually. I fell on my quivering knees, staring at him with red cheeks.

"Why..." my voice drifted. He pressed his forehead against mine, his gaze locking with mine. His dark eyes softened, and a mischievous curved on his lips.

"I was thirsty."

Chapter 13: Determinism

[**Determinism** /dəˈtɜrməˌnizəm/: *in philosophy, determinism refers to the theory that all events are completely determined by previously existing causes. Determinism is usually understood to preclude free will because it entails that humans cannot act otherwise than they do.*]

"Everything is determined, the beginning as well as the end, by forces over which we have no control. It is determined for the insect, as well as for the star. Human beings, vegetables, or cosmic dust, we all dance to a mysterious tune, intoned in the distance by an invisible piper."

-Albert Einstein

***

"Hey, Conan, do you want to help me pick some berries?" Zev asked when we returned to the cabin. "Freddie is knocked out on the couch and Adah went to the groceries."

"I still haven't unpacked," I frowned, still soaking wet.

"I'll take care of them," Parker reassured me. Before I could reply, he turned towards Zev. "Our room is on the second floor, right?"

Zev told us that Parker and I could share a room.

"Yeah, the first one on the left," he said, nodding towards the flight of stairs. Parker thanked him and swiftly picked up our heavy luggage, the muscles in arms and chest bulging when he did.

"Aren't they heavy?" I asked worriedly. Parker rolled his beautiful dark eyes and didn't bother answering the question.

"You don't mind if I unpack for you, right?" he said, already halfway up the stairs.

"No," I murmured. All I brought were some clothes and hygienic products. I also brought a philosophy book and my journal, but I doubted Parker would bother opening them. He wasn't a fan of literature. I once tried to convince him to read my favorite book written by Plato, but he fell asleep on the first page. He was sitting on the couch, his head tilted back and the opened book covering his eyes. I thought he was joking at first, but when I removed the book from his face, he was sound asleep.

He glanced over his shoulder, smiling at me. The glimmer of mischief twinkling in his dark eyes and the secretive glance he gave me reminded me of what he had done in the shed, and I felt my cheeks heat up immediately.

"I'll see you later," he said. I nodded, giving him a shy wave as I watched him disappear upstairs. When I turned towards Zev, I stiffened. He was wearing a grin too wide for his face.

"What?" I asked, and he laughed, shaking his head.

"Nothing, nothing," he said, but I knew there was something. I frowned, and he caved in. "You two just look so happy together. It makes me happy."

I smiled at his heartwarming words.

"Now, go take a shower. We have some berries to pick," he said, ushering me to the washroom. "Turn the faucet left for hot water and right for cold. The showers are on the top shelf. I'll grab you a dry pair of clothes."

I finished washing up and wore Zev's clothes which were two sizes too big. I looked like a kid wearing his father's clothes. When I stepped out of the showers, Zev looked at me and burst into laughter. He laughed so hard, he woke up Freddie, who was annoyed at first until he saw me, and then laughed as well. They told me how cute I was, and I blushed in embarrassment. Zev took a picture of me and refused to delete it.

We picked up the straw baskets and headed to a nearby forest to hunt for blueberries. He told me that he'd always come here with his grandma when he was younger, telling me how she'd make the best blueberry pies. He looked so young and happy when recounting his old childhood. I walked beside Zev and studied his profile as he spoke. He had a straight nose and sharp jaw, and the corners of his eyes would wrinkle when he smiled. His skin glowed a dewy gold under the sun. Zev was the light that brought life to Freddie, Parker, and my life. He was the happiest amongst us four. He was a lucky man with a loving family and girlfriend, and even though his life wasn't perfect, it wasn't a constant battlefield.

He brightened the mood whenever there was tension, and he'd make jokes and find ways to make us smile, and I couldn't thank him enough for existing. I felt indebted to his parents for creating such a beautiful being. I bet Zev was born smiling and would die the same way.

"There they are!" he exclaimed, pointing at the rows of high bushes ornamented with specks of blue. He plucked one off its branch and examined it carefully to make sure there weren't any bugs, before handing it to me.

"Here, try one," he said, grinning. I put it in my mouth. My eyes widened when it exploded between my teeth, and a sweet taste burst on my tongue. It tasted like sugar. Zev read the expression on my face and laughed that hearty laugh of his.

"It tastes like candy," I said.

"I know, right?" he said, picking three more and popping them into his mouth. We spent the rest of the afternoon picking and eating blueberries. We ate so many, we felt sick. Our baskets were full, so we decided to return to the cabin.

"I had lots of fun. Thank you for bringing me here," I said. "I can't wait to write about today in my journal."

"Do you write everything in it?" he asked curiously.

"Only the important stuff."

Zev smiled.

"Have you ever written a memoir?" I asked.

"No, I'm afraid I haven't. Why?"

"Because I want my journal to be a memoir, but I don't know how I should start or end it," I murmured, looking straight ahead.

"Well, if a memoir is a short biography of one's life, then maybe you should start from when you were born and end it right before you die?"

From when I was born... I pursed my lips, then shook my head.

"My life didn't start until I came to the Big City," I told him. Zev's eyebrows quirked up.

"If you start your memoir when you arrived at the Big City then when would it end?"

"I don't know yet." I paused. "I guess my memoir would end when I consider my life over. Life doesn't start when you're born, and death doesn't start when you're dead.

127

think one can very much be alive and dead, and dead but alive."

"How so?" he asked, and I nodded.

"We live through each other's thoughts and memories," I told him. "That's why I believe that me, you, Freddie, and Parker, the four of us, will live no matter what."

I looked at him and smiled.

***

When we returned to the cabin, Adah and Freddie gasped at the number of berries we collected. I noticed that Parker wasn't downstairs. Was he still unpacking? I headed upstairs to look for him. I couldn't wait to show him all the berries we picked. Zev said he'd bake us his grandma's blueberry pie, and I couldn't wait to try it. I smiled when I saw him in our room, but my smile vanished when I approached the door. Parker was sitting on the edge of the bed, his dark hair falling on his forehead. His hands were clenching something tightly, and my heart dropped to my stomach. He was holding my journal, and it was opened.

Parker didn't look up at me even though he knew I was here. He opened his mouth, closed it, tightened his jaw, and then finally spoke.

"I didn't mean to read it," he murmured, his voice hollow. My throat tightened, and I clenched my hands at my sides. "It fell out when I was unpacking and when I picked it up, it was opened to a page."

He looked at me with sorrow in his eyes. His pupils were black as a starless night. I kept gulping air, trying to breathe, but I felt my lungs tighten.

"What did I do wrong?" he croaked, his eyebrows pulling together. His eyes were bloodshot, and I realized he had been crying.

"What do you mean?" I asked, too shocked to feel anything else.

"Aren't you happy with me?"

The etch of pain in his voice made my chest tug.

"Of course, I am!"

"Then why the fuck am I sitting here reading a suicide letter?" he shouted angrily, his eyes filled with so much emotion. Betrayal, anger, frustration, and despair.

"What are you-" My eyes widened when the realization hit me. My journal must have fallen to the letter I had written months ago, the one I wrote after the incident with Ryan. It was when I had reached one of the lowest points in my life. But that was before Parker and I talked. It was before I realized that my life didn't have to be a clump of misery as long as I had Parker and my friends. But I never wrote the date on the pages. Parker didn't know when I wrote that letter. All he saw were lines saying that I was leaving.

"Why didn't you tell me?" he demanded. He was holding the journal so tightly, the pages wrinkled in his trembling hands.

"It's not what you think," I said, but Parker wouldn't listen. I flinched when he raised his voice.

"If you were so fucking miserable with me, why didn't you tell me?!" he shouted so loudly, my bones shook. "You were never going to stay, were you? You told me we'd be happy together, you said we'd have a future with each other, you made so many promises, but they were all lies!"

I flinched at his harsh words, and my stomach twisted. He was slowly ripping my heart apart. I tried to say something, but he beat me to it. His voice fell to a miserable whisper, rough and ragged.

"I tried so hard, Conan, I gave you everything I could. Was I not enough? Why-" he couldn't finish his sentence. Parker was crying. I knew he couldn't think rationally when he was angry, and I frantically tried to think of something that would calm him down, but I realized at that fatal moment that people didn't change. Parker couldn't control his emotions, and I would never function like a normal person. If I were Zev or Freddie, I would have known what to say, but I was Conan, the broken man who couldn't put his thoughts into words. And right now, my mind was a haze and my brain a glitch.

"Parker, I'll explain everything," I uttered in a rush, trying to collect my jumbling thoughts. "I just need some time to think. Please listen to me, it's not what you think."

But the misunderstanding broke his trust.

"You were going to leave no matter what I did." His voice was empty.

My eyes stretched open.

"That's not true!" I pressed, and he laughed such a morbid laugh, I felt a blade twist into my heart. His laugh faded, and all that was left was an expression of immense grief. His gaze held mine.

"If only we had never met."

He didn't finish his sentence, but he didn't need to. My heart split into two, and Parker stormed past me, his strong shoulders almost knocking me over.

"Parker! Parker, wait!" I shouted desperately, running after him. I caught his arm, but he pulled away with so much force, I fell on my thin knees. He didn't stop or look over his shoulder. I scrambled onto my feet, ignoring the pain that jolted up my legs at each step.

"Parker!" I cried with tears in my eyes, trying to stop him, but he grabbed his keys and headed out the door without his helmet. He climbed onto his motorcycle, and I screamed his name, but my voice was drowned by the loud engines that roared to life, and before I could reach him, he was already gone.

Chapter 14: Dear

Dear,

Everything was going so well, but I had forgotten that life was unfair. Life was cruel and owed us nothing. It spared us no guilt.

Perhaps the light I saw in your eyes distracted me from reality. Though I didn't regret a second of that illusion, even if it hurts now, I don't regret it. The only regret I had was not being enough for you, Parker.

You had your own problems, your own traumas, your own demons and struggles; but you always took care of me first. I'm sorry I couldn't do the same. I'm sorry, I'm sorry, I'm sorry.

No matter how hard one tries, fate has our futures written in the stars. Trying to rearrange the comets would be as ridiculous as mankind trying to play God. But if humans were born so powerless, why did the Superior Beings not spare us even an inch of happiness?

If the world was infinitely large, and humans miserably small, why were we doomed to live miserably?

Parker calls me Dandelion. He loves the nickname, and so do I, but the reason behind its roots is a sad one. He told me he was afraid if he looked away for even a second, the wind would take me away and turn me into a million particles beyond his grasp.

Little did he know, little did I know, I would be the one to watch Parker drift away first.

Yours Truly

***

I was alone in our bedroom when the phone rang. It had been six hours since Parker had left. Zev and Adah went out looking for Parker. They wouldn't let me go with them, saying I should stay in the cabin in case he came back. Freddie stayed with me, but I asked him if I could be alone, and despite his reluctance, he hugged me tightly and told me he'd be in the living room.

Night had fallen. The weather was warm and it wasn't a day you'd expect to hear tragic news, but when I heard Freddie's frantic footsteps climb up the stairs, some part of me knew.

My throat was painfully dry and my hands were clammy. My heart raced and my stomach twisted, and my limbs felt weak, and my organs felt like they were shrinking beneath my bones, and I thought to myself at that very moment: this is what it must feel like to die a slow and painful death.

I tried to prepare myself during the last few seconds I had, but how did one prepare themselves for a tragedy? You simply couldn't. Freddie pushed open the door, tears in his eyes. His hand was tightly clenched around his phone, his knuckles were ghostly pale. My heart dropped to my stomach.

"Conan," he choked on my name, tears dripping down his face. "Parker, he-"

Freddie couldn't finish his sentence and crumbled to the floor. He pressed his forehead against the floor while his fingers curled, and he started to cry.

I sat there, unable to breathe.

And despite not knowing, I knew.

Chapter 15: The Crash

Parker got into a motorcycle crash.

He didn't do anything wrong and respected the speed limit. Ironically, it was a drunk driver that smashed into him at an intersection, and the impact sent Parker flying in the air. He wasn't wearing a helmet and when gravity pulled him down, he cracked his skull against the cement.

A week had passed since the accident. We weren't allowed to visit Parker who was still undergoing treatment in the emergency room. We weren't sure how critical his injuries were, nor if he'd survive. We didn't know anything.

Every day felt like an eternity. I felt like I was living in a void, and that life had become this dark hole, darker than it was before. I lost all sense of time and place. I lied in bed, staring at the ceiling, knowing that Parker wasn't above, and cried. I replayed our conversation, crying because it might have been our last, remembering the sorrow in his eyes and the pain on his face. I caused him to suffer, and I would never forgive myself. When I couldn't fall asleep, I'd look through our pictures and stare at my phone, looking at the digital pixels that replicated his face, pretending that he was lying next to me, smiling just like in the picture. But I missed the real Parker. I missed the smiling Parker, the scowling Parker, the loving Parker. I missed his touch, his gaze, his scent. Unable to bear his absence, I went to the mall the next day and bought Parker's cologne. When I returned home, I sprayed my sweater with it and pressed the fabric against my nose. The scent was there, but not his warmth, but it was the best I could do. I fell asleep that night hugging my sweater against my chest.

When I woke up, it was cold. It was no longer winter, and the sun was out, but I was shivering. I didn't go to university and stayed in bed, holding my sweater that had Parker's scent while reading our old messages. I smiled and laughed and cried as I read them. If only I hadn't written in my journal that day, if only I wrote the date, if only I could have communicated my thoughts better, maybe Parker would still be here. I hated the word 'if' and 'maybe,' and I hated the word 'hate.' But I hated myself more than I hated those three words, so I kept using them. Hate, hate, hate.

I forced myself to eat. I ate as much as I could, and even if I felt sick, I'd keep eating.

'You have to eat something,' I could hear Parker's voice echo inside my mind.

'I know, but I'm not hungry,' I replied.

'Just one more bite. Please, for me?'

Imaginary Parker would lean forward and kiss my forehead. I took another bite of my food, tricking myself into believing that if I finished my meal, I'd wake up from this terrible nightmare and find Parker lying beside me in my bed. Of course, that didn't happen.

I was so miserable that the Dark Thoughts took pity on me and left me alone. A different voice punished me instead. The Dark Thoughts tried to deform reality and blame me for things that weren't my fault, but the New Thoughts, the more painful ones, only spoke the Truth. The New Thoughts used 'if, maybe, hate,' and emphasized all my faults. It was my fault Parker was in so much pain. It was my fault Parker was so angry that day. It was my fault he didn't take a helmet. It was my fault he got into a motorcycle crash. I missed the Dark Thoughts.

I took the Emergency Pills prescribed by Dr. George Philip and even took sleeping pills. One night, I took so many, I woke up hours later with a dried mouth and a terrible headache. Part of me wished I had never woken up, but another part was glad that I did. If Parker was here, he would have hated me if I hadn't woken up, and I would have hurt him again. Thank God I didn't die. Thank God, thank God, thank God.

I lied in bed one night, realizing that this was the pain Parker must have suffered every day. He had lost someone he loved before and forced himself to continue living despite his loss, and I realized how much pain he had kept to himself. He rarely ever spoke of Eden, but despite rarely speaking of him, he thought about him every day. Parker suffered alone, and that made me cry.

And so, my life became a constant hunt to find methods to keep me alive. I tried smoking, but choked and vomited, and I had to eat an extra meal that day to recompense the food I threw up. Another day, when Parker's hospital still hadn't contacted me despite my numerous calls, I tried drinking alcohol. I drank half a bottle of vodka on my own, and I fell extremely ill. I couldn't walk properly, so I had to crawl up the dirty stairs to Freddie's door. The alcohol made it hard to remember what happened that day, but I couldn't forget the shocked look on Freddie's face when he saw me on the floor.

He helped me into his house and took care of me. He thought I was dying (which I was but not in the same way he thought), and he tried to call the hospital. I begged him not to, saying that if he did, they'd take me away forever, and that I would never be able to see Parker again. I slurred my words, and the headache was unbearable, but despite hating the feeling of being incapable of controlling my limbs and mind, I understood why people were addicted to toxic substances. I fell asleep weeping in Freddie's arms, knowing that despite the excruciating pain, it wasn't enough to kill me, and that I'd eventually wake up again.

Zev came over the next day. He found me kneeled in front of the toilet seat in Freddie's house, puking out my organs. Of course, it was a metaphor, but it didn't feel like one. He sunk to the floor beside me, studying my face ghostly pale complex with pained eyes, his lips slightly parted as if he wanted to say something but didn't know what to say. If he asked me if I was okay, or if I needed help, or if he could call 911, or if or if or if, I thought I'd lose my mind. But he hugged me tightly and cried. It was the first time I've ever seen Zev cry. Smiling, laughing, happy Zev was sobbing. I never drank an ounce of alcohol again.

I didn't know how much time had passed, but there was a knock at my door. My eyes flung open and I sprinted to the door so quickly, I nearly tripped on my way. When I opened the door, my heart dropped in disappointment. It was Freddie. His orange hair looked drained of color; they almost looked brown.

He must have read the disappointed look on my face, knowing that I was expecting Parker, because he said, "I'm sorry."

"It's okay." My voice was as empty as his.

"I got a call from the hospital. We can see Parker," he said, and I felt my heart race inside my chest. I felt both relieved and nervous. Visitation hours meant that Parker was still alive, but the sadness in Freddie's eyes made me anxious.

"I'll drive," I said, grabbing my car keys and heading for the stairs, but Freddie caught my wrist.

"Conan, there's something you should know before we go," he whispered, pain edging his voice. I tightened my hands, gently pulling away from his grasp.

"No, not now. Please, not now. I don't think I can handle it," I said. Freddie opened his mouth but closed it, nodding once, and I realized as I ran down the flight of stairs that Freddie hadn't looked me in the eyes the entire time.

***

I drove as quickly as I could to the hospital. Zev was waiting for us in the waiting room, and although he tried to smile when he saw me, he had the same grim expression as Freddie.

"He's in F21," was the first thing he said to me. The three of us went to the fourth floor and found Parker's room. My heart banged against my rib cage, and my hands clenched tightly at my sides. I took in a tight breath and opened the door.

My eyes stretched open.

Parker was sitting upon a white bed. There were two big machines beside him, and tubes stuck in his body. There was a bandage wrapped around his head. His once olive skin looked as pale as a fish's belly, and his beautiful, dark hair had been shaved to a buzz cut. He was handsome nonetheless, but I knew they had shaved his head not because he wanted to, but so that they could treat the gash on the side of his head. He had bruises and scratches on one side of his face, and a cotton patch on his cheekbone. Parker's eyes were still as dark as midnight, but for some reason, they seemed unrecognizable. They didn't hold the light they once did. But he was alive. Parker was alive. I sprinted to his side and held his hand, carefully wrapping it around mine. Tears streamed down my face, but smiled.

141

"Parker," I whispered. He looked at me with a confused expression on his face as if I called him another person's names. My stomach curled as I gently squeezed his hand, hoping he'd scowl like he always did or call me dandelion. But something didn't feel right.

My heart stopped when he slowly pulled away from me, his eyes darting to Freddie before glancing back at me in confusion. He pursed his lips.

"I'm sorry," he said, and the polite tone of his voice confirmed that something was very wrong. He held my gaze as if he was searching for something, but when he couldn't find the answer, he finally spoke:

"Who are you?"

Chapter 16: Departure

Parker couldn't remember me. The doctor told us that Parker suffered a severe head concussion. He lost some of his memories, but not all of them. From what we've been told, he remembered everything up to his early high school years, but everything after that was blank, which meant that Parker remembered Freddie but not me or Zev. He also didn't remember Eden, who he met during his late years in high school. The doctors told us that there was a small chance Parker would regain his memories and that we shouldn't act panicked in front of him.

I couldn't realize that I was now a stranger to Parker. After that day, I couldn't muster up the courage to visit him. The doctors told us not to act stressed or panicked, or show any behavior that would distress Parker, but I didn't know if was capable of retaining my emotions. Even though didn't go into his hospital room, I went to the hospital every day. Something about being in the same building as Parker comforted me. I'd stay in the waiting room before going to class and read books or do my homework. Nurses and doctors would come by and ask me why I was here, but they eventually stopped asking.

I went to see Parker when Freddie was with me.

"You're looking better," Freddie smirked. Parker saw him and smiled. The smile on his face shocked me. He'd normally scowl whenever he saw Freddie. He didn't even spare me a glance.

"The nurses take good care of me," he shrugged coolly, and Freddie rolled his eyes. "Though, the doctors here are kind of creepy. I can't wait to leave this place."

"And when's that?"

"Not for another two months," he said. "But ever since I woke up, I feel like a heavy burden has been removed from my shoulder as if I've woken up from a nightmare or something."

Parker then noticed that I was standing behind Freddie, and raised his eyebrows.

"You never introduced me to your friend," Parker said, and I stiffened. "He was here the last time, right?"

Freddie pulled me to his side, giving my arm a gentle squeeze.

"This is Conan," he said. "We live in the same building. He's our downstairs neighbor."

I could tell that Freddie wanted to say more, but the doctors warned us not to give information that might startle Parker. Parker looked at me and smiled. My chest hurt when he did. His smile wasn't the one I once knew. It was the type of smile you gave strangers.

"Hey, Conan. I'm Parker," he said. "Apparently, I'm your upstairs neighbor. Sorry if I don't remember much. I hit my head pretty hard."

The pain in my chest worsened. Parker rarely smiled and laughed, and now he was doing it so often, it didn't feel he wasn't Parker, but someone else. A stranger.

But the constant sorrow and pain that hung over his shoulders were gone. Now, he seemed happier, as if his amnesia had freed him from the memories that haunted him. The traumas that once weighed in his heart had vanished. The Dark Parker was gone, and he was now the Happy Parker.

"The tall guy from before, is he our neighbor too?" Parker asked, glancing back at Freddie. The subject changed so quickly, I couldn't help but feel disheartened.

"Uh, no, that was Zev. He's a friend of ours from college. Our best friend," Freddie murmured.

"Best friend? Shit, now I feel bad," Parker grumbled.

I quietly listened while Parker and Freddie chatted. They brought up old memories from their early years in high school. I got to learn more about Parker. He liked going out with his friends, and he dated quite a few girls bu never a boy. At least, not at that moment of his life. He excelled in school, always ranking first in bio-chem. He was popular, he was loved, he was happy. Parker was happy, happy, happy.

"Do you remember that time I snuck into the girl's bathroom to make-out with Helen?" Parker said, with an unfamiliar smirk on his face.

"Ugh, I do. You called me because one of the girls complained to the principal saying that someone was making unholy noises in one of the bathroom stalls," Freddie grumbled. Parker nodded eagerly and laughed.

"And you had distracted the principal in the hallway saying that you were in love with her," he cackled. "What did you tell her?"

"That age didn't matter and that I'd wait an eternity for her," Freddie sighed, but he joined Parker when he laughed. I felt so alone.

The doctors told us that visitation hours were over and that Parker needed to take his meds and get some rest.

"See ya, redhead," he grinned. He gave me a polite smile again. "Bye, Conan."

It should have been, 'Bye, Dandelion.'
"Goodbye, Parker," I replied, but he didn't hear me.

***

I went to visit Parker the next day without Freddie. I knocked on the door and opened it. Parker raised his eyebrows in surprise, his eyes quickly searching for someone. He expected Freddie to come with me. His eyes returned to mine, and he masked his surprise with a smile.

"Hey, neighbor," he said. I hated the new nickname. It meant nothing to me.

"Good afternoon, Parker," I said, swallowing the lump in my throat. I pulled out the chair beside his bed and sat down. I unzipped my bag, ignoring his stare.

"I brought you some books about art and philosophy," I said, trying to sound upbeat.

"No bio-chem?" he asked, surprised when I took out a stack of books.

"You don't like bio-chem."

Parker looked confused.

"How..." his husky voice trailed.

"You once told me," I informed him. He nodded.

"I've been getting a lot better," I told him. He seemed confused. "I've been eating three meals a day and I bought some books about food and cooking. I carry around nuts because they're high in calories and contain good fat. I'm getting better."

Words filled the air but they felt empty and meaningless, but I told him words that would have once meant something to him.

"And Zev has a dog and he lets me walk it some time so I also get to work out a little. I've also been studying hard for my exams and I asked some people who take the same classes as you for their notes. I copied them down so all you have to do is look at them."

I could tell that it was awkward and that I was making him uncomfortable. He didn't know what to say.

"Thank you," was all he said. I pressed my lips together, holding back the tears.

"I made you a turkey sandwich," I said, taking out the sandwich from my bag. "You're not vegetarian, are you?"

But only I understood the joke.

"No, I don't believe I am."

I placed the turkey sandwich and stood up.

"I'm going to leave now," I said.

"You can stay if you want."

I shook my head. It hurt too much.

He didn't insist, but I could feel his eyes on my back when I left. I closed the door behind me and crouched down, pressing my forehead against my knees.

Parker was gone, but he was happy.

Perhaps it was time for me to leave too.

Chapter 17: Freedom

I pulled my luggage from under my bed and started packing. I folded my clothes, stacked my journals, and put the rest of my belongings inside. But my hands stopped on a photo album Zev had given me a few weeks ago. When I asked him why he gave me a gift at such a random hour and random time, Zev said there wasn't always a reason behind gifts. He gave it to me simply because he wanted to. When I opened the album, there was a photo of me, Parker, Freddie, and Zev in our university's parking lot. The next one was of me and Parker on our apartment rooftop. I flipped the page and looked at the pictures we took during Christmas. There were bright lights, wide smiles, strangers that became my closest friends... As I continued flipping through the album, I realized that I couldn't let Parker go. It was selfish of me. I once said that all I wanted was Parker's happiness, and trying to bring him back would contradict my sole wish, but wasn't he happy when he was with me? Despite the pain, despite the suffering, despite the struggles, beyond the misery I brought him, didn't he find an ounce of happiness? I reached the last page where there was a sentence written in cursive.

Dear Conan,

If there's one thing I've realized, it's that everyone is incredibly damaged, so unbelievably torn, as if we were born to suffer immensely. And yet, we find reasons to live. When you finish flipping through this album, I hope you find more than one. I want you to know something: life is nothing but moments.

All these moments and feelings and people combine to make up a bigger moment that we call life. This album represents a small portion of your life, but I believe that in these few moments that were captured, you were happy. I hope you look back at these photos one day and realize how loved you are. No matter how beautiful or tragic a moment is, it always ends. So hold on a little tighter, smile a little bigger, cry a little harder, laugh a little louder, forgive a little quicker, and love a whole lot deeper because these are the moments you will remember when you're old and wishing you could rewind time. Not a single thing lasts forever but know that you were happy. So was I. These photos are proof of it.

The universe is incredibly big, and humans tragically small, but the world is ours.

Yours Truly

I didn't know who had written it since it wasn't signed. I could have been Parker, Freddie, Zev, or maybe the three of them.

I quickly wiped the tears from my face and closed the album. I grabbed my backpack and put the album and my journals inside. These items were proof that we existed, and I was going to show them to Parker.

I drove to the hospital and dashed to Parker's room. My heart frantically pounded against my ribcage as I sprinted down the white hallway, adrenaline pumping through my vines. I had to make Parker remember. We promised a future together: the mailbox with our names, the house we'd live in, the puppy we'd adopt, the good and bad days, the years we'd spend together...

I turned around the corner, and my eyes widened in surprise when I saw Parker's dad standing in front of Parker's room. He looked like he was looking for someone. His dark eyes met my gaze, and I had a feeling that the person he was looking for was me. I slowed down and walked up to him, panting.

"Hello, Dr. Anderson," I said. He pressed his lips together. He had dark circles under his eyes, and for the first time, he truly looked his age. Dr. Anderson looked older and tired as if life had caught up to him and wore him down.

"Conan," he spoke. "How have you been? I'm sure you were pretty shaken up after hearing the news about Parker."

I nodded. "Yes, but I'm trying my best for him."
I didn't clarify what, why, or how, but Dr. Parker seemed to understand.

"I know you share a special relationship with Parker. I've known since the day you bumped into him in my clinic.

I've only seen him get so upset about someone only twice in his life. Once was for his ex-boyfriend, and the second time was for you," he said, his voice low and husky. Dr. Anderson's jaw tightened, and he seemed hesitant, as if he wanted to tell me something but didn't know how to do it.

"My son," Dr. Anderson said, and he spoke both with great pride and sorrow. His dark eyes darkened with so much emotion that my chest twisted. I've only seen Dr. Anderson at his clinic when he put on a professional mask and spoke with a poker face. But right now, standing in front of me wasn't Sir Anderson the doctor, but Mr. Anderson, Parker's father. People hide their feelings so often that you sometimes forgot that they were human too.

"My son has been through a great deal of pain since he was little. He grew up without a mother, and no matter how hard I tried, I knew I couldn't fill that hole in his life. He's had behavioral issues since he was a kid. His therapists told me that the absence of a parent puts children at psychological risk, and Parker was emotionally unstable because of it. I'm not openly affectionate or loving, and I was harsh and cold towards Parker when I should have been more understanding. But I suffered greatly after my wife passed away, and I was left with a son I didn't know how to take care of."

Mr. Anderson's voice was strained, and he spoke as if he was on the verge of tears. His jaw tightened and unclenched.

"He met a wonderful friend in elementary school. Freddie played a big role in his life. He's smart and ambitious, but he has a motherly side to him. I don't know how the two of them became friends, but I'm grateful that they did

Freddie has always kept an eye on Parker and keeps him out of trouble. Back then, I thought I was pathetic. An eight-year-old boy was taking better care of Parker better than his own father. Things were getting better for Parker. He worked on his anger issues, threw fewer tantrums, got into less trouble, and I thought he was finally getting better; I thought his future was looking brighter," Mr. Anderson said. "And then he met Eden."

My chest tightened.

"Eden was a bright boy that everyone loved, and although he passed away too soon, I can still remember the smile on his face. When he died, Parker was heartbroken, and I knew he'd never recover from his death. I knew because even I couldn't get over my wife's death. Parker began throwing tantrums again, and his anger issues were uncontrollable. He found new and more toxic ways to numb his pain, and his entire life went spiraling. But this time, it wasn't Freddie who saved him, but you."

He looked at me with sad eyes but smiled.

"Conan, you've made Parker so happy," he said, and tears pricked my eyes. I tightened my fists at my sides, but I couldn't stop the pain from blossoming inside my chest. "And I know you want him back, but Parker is my son. He's all I have. You understand that, don't you?"

"What are you saying, Mr. Anderson?" I asked.

"No matter how good you were to him, you couldn't erase his pain, but now Parker can finally be happy. He's been freed from a tragic past and from the memories that haunted him. He's been freed from Eden's ghost. He can start fresh. He doesn't have to suffer anymore. He can finally live."

I stared at him, speechless.

"I know what you're going to do. You're going to try and make Parker remember you, but if you do, he might remember Eden too. I know you want him back, and that you feel wronged for being forgotten, but this is his chance to be happy. You've noticed, haven't you? How he smiles more, how he laughs, and how much brighter he is?"

I wanted to argue, but Mr. Anderson was right. I couldn't sense the sadness I once did when I saw Parker. But I didn't want to be forgotten. What would happen to me? How would I live on without him?

"I'm sorry, I need to tell him," I said, but when I reached to open the door, Mr. Anderson got on his knees and held my hand. Tears streamed down his face.

"Please," he begged me so quietly, so desperately. "Please free my son. Set him free so that he can be happy. I'm begging you, I'll do anything. Please, just let him go."

He held my hand so tightly, it hurt, but I didn't think he realized. Mr. Anderson was too preoccupied with his own pain.

"Let him be happy."

I wanted so badly to walk past Mr. Anderson and see Parker. He was only a few steps away. There was nothing but a thin door that separated us, yet my limbs wouldn't move. All I've ever wanted for Parker was for him to be happy. The conversation I had with him replayed in my mind.

'Would you think I'm a jerk if I said I was thinking about Eden? I was looking at the audience and I saw all these people sitting down, and I couldn't help but wish he was amongst them. It's stupid, I know. How can a dead person come back to life? But that didn't stop me from hoping. I want to tell him how much I miss him, and that even though he's no longer here, I still look for him, constantly, unconditionally. And that the world is painfully lonely without him, and that it'll never be the same no matter what I do.'

My lungs felt like they were closing inside my rib cage.

'I'm forgetting someone I can't forget. It's like he's dead but not entirely. Where does that leave me? And I'm caught between being happy and him. I wish he'd set me free. I wish someone would set me free.'

I wanted my mind to stop remembering, but I could never forget Parker.

'Would you believe me if I said I'm in so much pain, I could die?'

Mr. Anderson pressed his forehead against my hand, bringing me back to reality. His entire body shook, tears falling below him.

"Set him free," he rasped in desperation. "Let my son be happy again."

Chapter 18: A Day Like Any Other

It was June now. Spring was over and summer has begun. I called Freddie and Zev and asked if they could come over. They didn't ask any questions and came to my house. We spent the day watching movies and eating Zev's candies, laughing and chatting, and even went out for an afternoon stroll in the neighborhood park. When we returned home, we made dinner together and ate dinner. It was a day like any other, but something inside me told me that they knew. But Freddie and Zev ignored their instincts that day, masked their suspicion, and didn't ask any questions. Deep down, I guess they already knew.

After we finished our desserts — a delicious apple pie that Zev baked — we went to the apartment rooftop. But this time, we didn't climb up the emergency escape, and took the flight of stairs. We stood on the ledge and looked down at the city lights. The world was so beautifully dark, just like him.

We wrote letters to each other and decided to read them aloud. It was Zev's idea, and Freddie said it was a silly thing to do, but I noticed that he was holding onto his letter so tightly, the paper wrinkled in his grip.

"I'll go first," Zev said, unfolding the piece of paper in his pocket. He didn't face us, but the Big City. "Dear Friends," he began. "There are certain people we meet in our life who we connect with more than anyone else. You are those people. Thank you for loving me. Thank you for letting me love you. Thank you for letting me be part of your lives, no matter how long or short they are or will be, thank you. I'm sure that in some strange parallel universe afar, the four of us are together like in this one. In another universe, a man named Conan is living happily on a small hill, reading books and writing philosophy. He is a man without scars or trauma; a man who is treated fairly by the world. In another universe, there is a man named Freddie who is never mistreated or hurt."

Freddie turned his face away and started crying.

"He is somewhere out there living with a kind boyfriend who he'll adopt two cats with. In another universe, Parker still remembers us, and he's nagging and scowling at us because he doesn't know how else to express his love, but that's okay. He doesn't have to. We already know. We've always known. In another universe, life is fair, and the four of us are together, laughing that in some other world we're not. Yours truly, Zev."

Freddie quickly wiped away the tears on his face and unfolded his letter.

"Dear Zev, you are one of the best people I've met. You smile and laugh and are so kind. Reality is harsh, and the world is so scary, and we've found shelter in your brightness. Thank you for smiling when we couldn't, and thank you for giving us a reason to smile. Dear Conan," Freddie swallowed the lump in his throat. "Conan, you are too good for this world. This damn world that doesn't know a thing, because if it did, it wouldn't have treated you so unfairly. I hope Karma bites back and the world burns in flames. Damn it."

Tears dribbled off his chin and his letter shook in his hands.

"God damn it," Freddie choked. "God damn this world. Conan, you are the most selfless, kindest, most wonderful human being to exist. You are human. You are more human than humans themselves. Thank you for everything you taught me. Thank you for everything you taught us. Your words, your philosophy, your kindness... You are my friend, my brother, my family. Conan being Conan. Please never change."

My eyes widened at the phrase Parker used to always say.

"Yours truly, Freddie."

We looked up at the empty sky, hoping to see a shooting star to make a wish, hoping for a miracle. We kept searching and searching, because that's what humans do. They lived a life full of pain and misery, but hoped.

We cried that night. We cried our hearts out, for everything we've been robbed of, for everything that could have been, for every pain and suffering we've been through. We cried because we felt too much, because we were friends, because we loved and were loved. We cried for Parker. Oh, our dear Parker.

We cried because we were human.

Chapter 19: The Last Entry

I finished packing my luggage. I carried them down the creaky stairs and went down to the first floor, stopping at the twin doors. I looked over my shoulder and smiled at the broken elevator and then glanced at the tape outlining a corpse, remembering the first day I entered the apartment I was going to miss this place.

I left and went to the parking lot, heading to my car.

"Conan!" Someone shouted. It was Parker. He jogged up to me with a smile on his face. He was released from the hospital a month ago. His hair was starting to grow and you could no longer see the scar on the side of his head. He was handsome, but inside he was beautiful. He ran a hand through his hair, and I glanced at his beautiful forehead. Parker frowned when he noticed the luggage at my side, and his dark eyes met my gaze.

"Are you moving out?" He asked.

I nodded. "I am."

"Where are you going?"

"Not far away."

He raised his brows but nodded.

"Well, good for you. Nothing good will come out of staying in this old, crappy building. Anyway, if you ever have time, don't hesitate to come back and say hi."

"How have you been doing?" I asked.

"Better," he smiled, and I knew he meant it.

"I'm glad," I smiled, and I really was.

He pursed his lips, looking deeply into my eyes as if he was searching for something. My heart raced inside my chest. Parker opened his mouth to say something, but a loud honking broke our gaze. A red car drove into the parking lot.

"That's my ride," he said, looking strangely disappointed. "My motorcycle's been completely crushed so my friends have been driving me here and there. I have to get going. Take care of yourself, yeah?"

He looked at me, held my gaze, and smiled.

"I'll see you later," he said.

I waved at him, watching him jog to the car. He slipped into the passenger's seat. His friend said something, and Parker rolled his eyes but smiled. She leaned towards him and ran a hand through his hair, laughing. They left the parking lot.

I put my luggage in the trunk and climbed into my car. I drove out of the Big City, glancing at the blurry buildings and people on the streets. The City Bus stopped in front of me at the red light, and I smiled as the memories floated in my mind. As I drove further away, the tall buildings began to disappear, and the cars started to disappear. Something caught my eye. I parked my car beside a field of dandelions, my eyes widening at the millions of fluffy flowers dancing in front of me. I watched them sway back and forth. They looked like they were waving at me. As if the dandelions were calling me to finally join them, I walked into the field. I sat down on a small patch of green grass, surrounded by flowers, and took out my journal, and began writing.

Dear,

The rest of the day and the ones to follow will go normally as expected. It is a day like any other. Something has been altered, but the world will continue moving forward. I once told you that I wrote for you. From beginning to end, this story was never about me. It is about my friends. It is about Parker. It is proof that we existed, and that we will continue existing.

I'm glad that even if it was temporary, I had found a home, a family, and someone that I love. I'm glad that you didn't say goodbye to me, Parker. I'm glad that we didn't part on a definite goodbye because it means we never left each other.

Life is going to be hard. You are going to make mistakes, you are going to fall, and you are going to feel like it's the end of the world, but you are going to stand up and keep living because you are going to be happy. You may never read this last letter, but I hope that whenever you see a dandelion, instead of plucking it off its stem to make a wish, I hope that you think of me or at least a fragment of what we were, but most of all, I hope you look at it and smile.

Yours Truly

Made in the USA
Middletown, DE
16 June 2021